Macro Mayhem

Macro Mayhem

A Dia Fenner Economic Thriller

Michael L. Walden
and
M. E. Whitman Walden

iUniverse, Inc.
New York Lincoln Shanghai

Macro Mayhem
A Dia Fenner Economic Thriller

iUniverse books may be ordered through booksellers or by contacting:

iUniverse
2021 Pine Lake Road, Suite 100
Lincoln, NE 68512
www.iuniverse.com
1-800-Authors (1-800-288-4677)

ISBN-13: 978-0-595-38000-8 (pbk)
ISBN-13: 978-0-595-82371-0 (ebk)
ISBN-10: 0-595-38000-X (pbk)
ISBN-10: 0-595-82371-8 (ebk)

Printed in the United States of America

To the thousands of students and other learners we have taught. You inspired us.

ACKNOWLEDGMENTS

Several friends, colleagues, and family members read the manuscript and made constructive comments, including Bob Campbell, Gayle Horton, David Hyman, Shirley Ihnen, Loren Ihnen, John Lapp, Penn Pace, Janice Raish, Tiffany Tyler, and Nancy Whitman. They deserve our sincere thanks for improving the project without contributing to any of its faults. We also thank the editorial staff of iUniverse for their expert service.

1. FIRST FEAR

Dia just couldn't shake the vehicle behind her. Every turn she made, it made. The headlights tracked her like a prowling cat. She purposefully passed open spaces in the multitiered parking deck, but the pursuer kept pace and followed. Even though it was still unseasonably warm at almost 10:00 PM, a cold sweat began to appear on her brow. After all, in every movie she'd ever seen, nothing good ever happened in dark, deserted parking decks!

Dia was running out of levels; plus, she was tired. Always one to take the initiative, she decided to bring the chase to an end. She turned in to the next open space, pulled out her cell phone, and dialed 911. With her finger poised to press the call button, she nervously watched the predatory vehicle come to a stop. A figure hidden by the darkness emerged from the vehicle and approached her car. As Dia's eyes darted from the stranger back to her phone, the device slipped from her hand onto the car's floor. Nervously she fumbled for the phone but couldn't find it in the dark. As the predator drew closer, Dia wondered if her young life would come to an end here, in a city she had just recently moved to and that still seemed so big and foreign to her.

Heavy knuckles rapped on the passenger side window, and Dia jumped. The figure was now at the side of her car, talking.

"Dr. Fenner, I thought that was you," a voice shouted. "It's Hank, the night parking attendant." Feeling foolish but very relieved, Dia slumped back in her seat and exhaled.

"I hope I didn't scare you, but when you came through the gate I noticed you still hadn't received your garage parking sticker. The guy who comes in at five is a real stickler for rules, and if you don't have a sticker, he'll call to have your car towed. I know you're new to the building, and I didn't want you having problems right off the bat," Hank explained. "I have a temp sticker for you to use until you can get your permanent one from the management company."

Dia rolled down her window and managed to thank the grandfatherly attendant, all the while trying to slow the adrenaline rush still pulsing through her veins. Her emotions, coupled with the exhaustion of feeling her way through a new job and moving to an enormous city where she didn't know anyone, were taking their toll.

"Here," Hank said as he thrust a thin piece of plastic into Dia's now unclenched hand. "Put this on the lower right side of your front windshield." The helpful watchman turned, walked away to his car, and waved cheerfully as he drove away.

Dia rested her head on the steering wheel and took a deep breath. She made a mental note to add getting a parking sticker to her growing "to do" list. Apparently, Washington, D.C.'s, reputation as a city known for its paper-pushing bureaucratic rules was well deserved.

Lydia (Dia to her friends) Fenner had just received a PhD in economics from Cornell University. Her specialty was macroeconomics, the study of the national economy. She had considered several competitive job offers from universities, think tanks, and government agencies, before deciding to take the position of senior economist to the Assistant Secretary for economic policy at the U.S. Treasury Department.

It had been a difficult choice, but Dia took the Treasury job because D.C. was "where the action was" in macroeconomic policy. Dia now had a chance to influence and form the policies she had only been able to study in graduate school. This was heady stuff for a mere twenty-eight-year-old.

Tonight's parking deck trauma was just another example of how unsure Dia was in a big city. Washington was truly a metropolis, on par with Boston, Philadelphia, and even New York. It was light years removed from the small college town of Ithaca, New York, home of Cornell, or from tiny Chillicothe, Ohio, where Dia grew up. Right now she was really missing the easygoing pastoral environments of her former homes, where traffic jams, huge complexes of confusing buildings, and eerily lit, semidark parking garages hadn't been issues.

Walking wearily down a long hallway, Dia was relieved to open the door and safely lock herself inside her apartment. It was small by most standards but average for high-priced Washington real estate. Dia understood the economics of the housing market, which resulted in higher prices per square foot in cities with lots of amenities—restaurants, pro sports, stores—compared to small towns that were miles from anything. Dia's building was in a neighborhood popular with young professionals, and she was determined to take advantage of all those opportunities she was implicitly paying for. As soon as she got thoroughly settled in, she would start sampling some of the delis with mouthwatering aromas and browse the boutiques with the intriguing window displays. But these treats weren't going to happen this week.

Somewhat of a neat freak, Dia wasn't happy she hadn't had time to put everything away, even though she'd just moved in last week. Half unpacked boxes still cluttered her rooms. She had promised herself to do a little straightening up for a couple of hours each night after work. After the harrowing parking garage experience, she was too tired to do anything about it tonight. She'd only been on the job two days, but trying to make a good first impression had made them extra long days, and Dia was ready to collapse into bed.

A phone rang just as Dia was falling to sleep, startling her back to semiawareness. Reaching clumsily for her cell, she flipped the phone open. She was surprised to discover that the cell phone wasn't ringing; it was her landline. Dia was puzzled because she hadn't had time to give the number to anyone. Even her family didn't have it. In fact, on the advice of her Treasury superiors, she told the phone company not to list the number.

Who could be calling at this hour? It was probably a wrong number, or maybe it was "helpful" Hank calling because her car lights were on. He could have some kind of directory for getting in touch with parking garage renters. Wearily she lifted the receiver to her ear, all the while wondering if this nightmare of an evening was ever going to end.

2. HACKED

"Hello," Dia groggily answered.

"Dr. Fenner, I'm sorry to bother you at home at this hour, but this just couldn't wait," responded the voice on the other end of the line. As exhausted as she had been, she was now instantly wide awake.

Dia immediately recognized the caller as Adam Kasten, the Assistant Treasury Secretary for economic policy and her boss. Kasten was a Harvard MBA graduate and consequently, as economists were quick to say, he knew how to run businesses, but he didn't necessarily know how businesses ran. The latter, of course, was the expertise of economists. Kasten's job was to develop and evaluate macroeconomic policy options for the Secretary of the Treasury.

"Dr. Fenner, a report on the Chinese economy was just faxed here from our embassy in Beijing," Kasten continued. "I think you should look at it before tomorrow's nine o'clock meeting with the Secretary."

Annoyed, Dia wondered whether Kasten expected her to rush out of the apartment and drive back to work in the middle of the night. Fortunately, her brain cells kicked in just in time to bite back a rather insolent response. Her mother had always warned Dia about containing her quick temper.

"Thank you, sir. I'll make sure to come in early and study the report before the meeting."

"That will be fine, Dr. Fenner. Good night," Kasten answered in clipped, military cadence.

"Oh, Mr. Kasten, before you go, would you mind telling me how you got my number? It's unlisted, and I don't recall giving it to anyone at the office." Dia knew she was being rather forward, but in today's world, it was wise to be careful about both her safety and privacy.

"Dr. Fenner, there are ways to get all kinds of information in Washington if you know where to look," Kasten said with slight condescension in his voice. Click!

Sighing, Dia reset the alarm for an hour earlier than was previously set. In Chillicothe this would be called "getting up with the chickens." Planning to beat the usual D.C. traffic was bad enough. Now, she had yet another report to read before the meeting at nine. Being a firm believer that first impressions were as important as the old adage claimed, she aimed to come across as competent and worthy of her new position. If losing a few hours of sleep was what it took, then so be it. Dia was pretty sure this wouldn't be the only time it would happen, and she might as well get used to it now.

The U.S. Department of Treasury was established in 1789, making it the second oldest in the President's cabinet after the State Department. The Secretary of the Treasury (SOT) is fifth in line in the presidential succession. Befitting this status, the SOT's office overlooks the White House. It also happens to be magnificent! Rich mahogany wood is everywhere—walls, side tables, conference tables, and oversized desks and chairs. Much of the furniture is antique, acquired over decades by earlier Treasury secretaries with obvious good taste. The department's seal is artfully woven into the middle of the deeply plush, wool carpet. Elegant French chandeliers softly illuminate the imposing room, allowing each piece of furniture and every item on display to be seen at its best.

Dia was up at 4:30 AM and in the office before six to go over the Chinese report. She made all the appropriate changes in the notes she was expected to have ready for today's meeting. Taking a quick gulp of coffee, she chewed on the stale Danish she was grateful not to have finished yesterday. She made a face as she swallowed. Her mother was an excellent cook, and wonderful meals had always graced the table in Dia's childhood home. All through graduate school she had regretted not taking a bigger part in preparing the dinners, especially on the nights she resorted to fast food to save time for papers and research.

Sighing, Dia stood up from her desk and stretched. Checking her reflection in the long mirror hanging on the back of her office door, she decided she was presentable enough. Of course, it helped that her shoulder-length shiny black hair had a natural wave, and her slim figure maintained itself with virtually no thought beyond her lifelong love of athletics. Deciding she was "good to go," she gathered papers, left the office, and headed down the hall.

Thinking she'd be among the first to arrive, Dia was surprised to see several Treasury Department personnel already seated around the large conference room table. Dia took the empty chair next to Adam Kasten. Everything she'd heard about the movers and shakers in Washington always jockeying for position was proving to be true. She could feel the quick glances coming at her from all sides, assessing the "new kid" before she'd even had a chance to open her mouth.

As if by script, everyone settled and became quiet. A dramatic moment later, the Treasury Secretary entered the room. If you could order one from central casting, Lawrence Bowman looked the part of a Treasury Secretary. Tall, tan, distinguished, with a full head of thick gray hair, Bowman was a commanding presence. He was attired in a stylish, three-button dark blue Joseph Abboud suit and a crisp white shirt with monogrammed cuffs held together by sparkling silver cuff links. His one indulgence in color was a brightly patterned Tommy Hilfiger tie. Bowman made all heads turn when he entered any room.

Lawrence Bowman had been the CEO of the tech giant Cenitron Industries. He gained a reputation as a savvy executive when he guided Cenitron relatively unscathed through the boom-and-bust period of the late 1990s. During the election he was the President's chief fundraiser, and for his successful efforts at raising record amounts of cash, he had been awarded the Secretary of the Treasury post. Although the administration had multiple sources of economic advice, including the Council of Economic Advisors, Treasury Department, and the National Economic Council, Bowman was considered the President's chief economic spokesman.

"Team," Bowman started—he liked the team concept—"the President isn't happy with the economy. As you know, the President's party took a beating in the midterm elections, primarily because of the sluggish job market. We can do better. We *must* do better. Americans expect good-paying jobs, and this President is determined to give the American people what they want."

Like Adam Kasten, Bowman was a businessman, not an economist. In his position as head of the Treasury, he approached issues just as he did at Cenitron: identify the problem, put a team together to formulate a solution, and then solve the problem. It was as simple as that. He saw no reason why that tactic couldn't work with the national economy.

Bowman was standing and gesturing like a coach warming up the players for the big game. He spoke enthusiastically, drawing in everyone around. "Here are the problems that the President and I see. First, we're losing good-paying manufacturing jobs and replacing them with lousy service jobs. Unemployment is higher than when the President took office. And we're getting our butts kicked by cheap foreign labor. How in the world can our fifteen-dollar-an-hour workers compete with fifteen-cent-an-hour workers? It's just not fair."

Dia was surprised at Bowman's comments. She glanced around the room to see if anyone else indicated a similar feeling but saw only expressionless faces. Apparently Bowman's tone and content weren't new. What bothered Dia was the simplicity of the Secretary's remarks—almost like campaign slogans—and the generalized conclusions they drew. Yes, service jobs were increasing, but they certainly weren't universally low paying.

Warming up to his subject with his captive audience, Bowman was on a roll: "Second, we're borrowing money right and left for the budget deficit, and as a result, the President is getting dragged through the coals in the press for being fiscally irresponsible. After all, he ran on a platform of a balanced budget. Making matters even worse, our trade deficit is in the red, too."

The Secretary paused dramatically for a sip of water. Dia thought he probably would have preferred something stronger, even at this early hour. "To top it all off, inflation is down, but the President isn't getting any credit for this good news."

"Folks,"—Bowman shifted gears to a folksy manner after his tirade—"we need a plan to correct the course of our economic ship, and we need that plan *now*." Bowman pronounced the word "now" as if it were in capital letters. It was obvious this man was used to giving orders and having anyone within hearing range jump to respond.

Bowman directed his attention to Adam Kasten. "Adam, I want your office to take the lead in developing our stimulus plan." Including the rest of the group around the table in his gaze, he continued, "And I want each and every one of you to give Adam all the support he needs."

Kasten gave a smirking smile as he said, "Yes sir." Then Kasten turned to Dia and added, "And I'll have our new senior economist, Dr. Fenner, be the chief author of the plan."

Dia took a gulp and waved limply to her colleagues. It was uncomfortable enough when everyone was eyeing her every move surreptitiously. Kasten's pronouncement was like giving permission for all to abandon any pretense of subtlety and just stare blatantly at their new coworker and competitor for advancement. She didn't exactly feel hostility, but there weren't any warm smiles of support, either.

Bowman dismissed the group and quickly exited through the side door. No questions were asked or reports discussed. The sleep Dia had lost in reading and summarizing the new Chinese information had been for nothing. She expected Kasten to linger and discuss the stimulus plan in more detail, but he too left hurriedly without even acknowledging her.

As Dia walked down the hallway to her office alone, she thought more about what Bowman had said. His comments had really sounded more political than economic. It was as if he had grabbed statements from the headlines without doing any analysis. But then, what did she know? Maybe that's what Treasury secretaries did. Maybe she, Dia Fenner, was supposed to provide the analysis.

Back at her office, Dia continued to think about her new assignment when she suddenly stopped and stared at the screen of her computer. As a precaution, Dia had installed software she used in graduate school to record any attempts at illegally accessing her files. Now her screen was flashing a message that not only had someone tried to access a file, but they had successfully copied it. It was the file of the notes she had just finished this morning for the meeting with the Secretary.

There was also an e-mail message waiting. Dia went cold as she read it: "Dia, I've found you. Now I'll ruin you. I just have to decide when. Kyle."

3. STRIKE FORCE

The room was packed with computer monitors and TV screens. From their perch on the overlooking balcony, Michael Narone and Philip Casini watched activity swarming inside the high-tech hive.

"The information we're receiving suggests the time may be quite near." Narone spoke with satisfaction. It was difficult to tell whether his apparent pleasure came from the statement and all it implied or his enjoyment of the premium cigar he alternately pressed between his manicured fingers and his tight, controlling mouth.

"I know, I know, and everything's set," agreed Casini. "But I'm still not convinced this is the right move to make."

"I thought we settled all this," Narone answered shortly, anger flaring in his eyes. Realizing Casini usually appreciated a more logical argument, he continued more calmly: "We may not have this same opportunity for several years. If we act now, our target will be caught totally off guard."

"But the operation will be exceedingly expensive," Casini said, raising his voice above the chatter and electrical hum from below. He looked around to see if they were being observed and then tried once more to reason with Narone. "We could use these same resources to reach our objective in other ways."

Standing and slamming his fist on the railing, Narone commanded: "And I say the paper strike *will* occur. It's only a matter of when."

4. FRIEND OR FOE?

Graduate school had been almost nonstop work for Dia. She always demanded the best of herself, so she put in long hours at the library and gave up many enjoyable activities most college students routinely indulge in. It wasn't that she didn't like going clubbing or dating interesting men. She was simply willing to postpone those pleasures so she could complete her degree and land a challenging job. That was her goal.

There was one exception to her time spent on academic pursuits. Ever since starting her dissertation, Dia released her stress in the gym. Weight lifting followed by cardio work always seemed to decompress her. She was one of those people others often looked at curiously as she turned down social invitations to pass what little free time she allowed herself in the confines of iron, stainless steel, and weight collars. Exercise had another, more indulgent, benefit for Dia. It allowed her to enjoy the desserts she loved without their calories showing up in unwanted places.

Entering the Gold's Gym on Connecticut Avenue, Dia thought back to Kyle's sinister sounding message. Kyle had been Dia's boyfriend for the past two years. They were quite opposite in all ways that mattered. At first Dia found this charming. Kyle was her other half, the one that operated on an emotional overdrive that she never had. She was too pragmatic to take the right-brained approach to anything she considered mildly important.

Dia and Kyle broke up over Dia's decision to take the Treasury job in Washington. Kyle wanted them to move to a rural area where he could pursue his passion for organic farming. Dia's choice of D.C. was a deal breaker. Kyle initially tried to convince Dia she could use her degree online. Weren't there many jobs available where someone in her field could use all the high-tech wizardry at one's fingertips from a well setup home office? The more he argued, the harder Dia fought for control over what she had worked so long and so hard to achieve. It was as if his insistence on having his way drove a permanent wedge in their relationship. The words they exchanged at their final separation were cruel and ugly.

After completing a punishing bench press, Dia looked up to see someone staring at her from across the room. He looked vaguely familiar. She tried to place him. Had she seen him somewhere at work, or perhaps simply in passing at Gold's? As she puzzled over this, their eyes met, and the man began moving toward Dia. She was impressed with how confidently the stranger carried himself and noticed that others watched approvingly as he moved by.

"Hi, I'm Jim Sawyer. I work in the International Affairs Office at Treasury. I've seen you in the hallways and noticed you at the meeting this morning." As he talked, Jim stuck out his hand. He was so tall he had to lean over to get any place close to shaking her hand. Dia stood up from the bench to make things easier.

"Glad to meet you," Dia replied, smiling and taking Jim's outstretched hand. She couldn't help but admire her handsome colleague. She wondered if he realized how the blue in his shirt brought out the color of his eyes. As he pushed a mop of light brown hair away from his forehead, a well-exercised bicep contracted under the sleeve of his shirt.

"So you deal with international economics?" It was the best Dia could think of at the moment.

"Yeah, the standard stuff. I track exports and imports and the resulting national trade balance. Just as I learned in school, I see our imports jump and exports stumble when the dollar becomes stronger against foreign currencies, and imports grow slower and exports really take off when the dollar weakens. I also watch investment flows—you know—how much money foreigners are investing in the U.S. compared to how much we're investing in foreign countries. It's always amazing at the end of the year how net investment flows to the U.S. are virtually the mirror image of the difference between our exports and imports of products and services."

"I know. That was one of the hardest concepts for me to grasp as an undergraduate." She was happy to be able to combine two of her favorite activities—discussing economics and working out. "For example," Dia continued, "if foreigners are accumulating dollars because they're selling more to us than we're selling to them, then those dollars will eventually be invested back in the U.S. It's like we're trading stocks, bonds, and mutual funds for their products."

Almost on cue Jim added: "So our country may lose jobs from foreign-made imports being sold here, but new jobs are created when foreigners turn around and invest their dollars. Although it's logical, many politicians don't like to hear it."

Dia immediately liked Jim, and they obviously had a lot in common. Maybe her move to Washington and the start of a new life were on the upswing. She was beginning to forget her worries over Kyle and the file of notes stolen from her computer.

Eager to keep the conversation going, Dia asked, "Are you working on any particular projects now?"

"I have two job assignments right now," Jim said through reps of bicep curls. "One is to compare the pay and skills of jobs our country is losing to those we're gaining through increased international trade and foreign investment. Nine, ten...whew," Jim puffed.

Dia finished her next set while Jim was talking. "Any initial findings?" She was very interested in the topic.

"The majority of manufacturing jobs we're losing are lower paying ones," Jim said as he wiped his face with a towel. "The jobs we're gaining take advantage of our edges in equipment and technology and consequently pay more. Productivity is our ace in the hole. If our workers can produce twenty times more in an hour than foreign workers, then they'll actually be a bargain if they're only paid ten or fifteen times more."

"Why would anyone be upset if we're losing low-paying jobs and gaining higher paying ones?" Dia inquired.

Jim started to do some hammer curls. "First, I think the media always focuses on the bad rather than the good. But second, I don't think we've done a very good job of retraining those workers who have been displaced by international trade. Without upgrading their skills, they really have no other option than a low-paying service job."

Dia added weight for her heavy bench press. "What's the second thing you're dealing with, Jim?"

"I'm trying to measure the savings consumers are gaining by having access to lower-priced imported products," Jim said as he returned the twenty-five-pound dumbbells. "Already I've estimated people buying clothes are saving $20 billion a year by being able to purchase lower-priced, foreign-made apparel. So although some may complain about international trade, when consumers vote with their wallets, they appear to like it."

Dia was impressed. Not only did she and Jim have common interests in their respective fields in economics, but he appeared to be as diligent as she was about working out. She'd confirmed this as he talked, stealing a look at his well-formed muscles while she listened. Was this someone who could replace Kyle and make the big city seem friendlier?

"So, lucky you, being given the job of developing an economic policy plan for Bowman. Talk about having your feet immediately held to the fire," Jim teased with a wink of his eye.

"I know," Dia replied while stretching, "and I think I'll have a lot of educating to do in the process. The field of macroeconomics has been extremely fertile for new thinking in recent decades. It really all started with the combination of high inflation and high unemployment in the 1970s, which traditional macroeconomic theories couldn't explain. In the eighties we had the development of supply-side economics, and later came concepts like rational expectations, the real business cycle, and new Keynesian theory."

"Hold on, my head is spinning." Jim feigned dizziness. "That's too much for my feeble mind to take in all at once. We're just going to have to have several more meetings so you can bring me up to speed on the latest macroeconomic thinking!"

Dia couldn't help but blush as she looked forward to the idea of getting to know Jim Sawyer better.

Jim spotted Dia on her last set of bench presses. As she lowered the bar, she heard him pay her a compliment: "Say, I was impressed with the analysis of our bilateral trade with China you presented in the seminar for your job interview a couple of months ago. I agree China will steadily become a bigger and bigger market for our agricultural and high-tech products."

Dia froze and stopped the press midlift, losing all momentum and forcing Jim to help her get the bar back on the rack. Indeed, she had done a trade analysis of China. But it wasn't for her job interview. It was in the notes she had finished only this morning for the meeting with Bowman. And she hadn't given her notes to anyone; they were only for her reference. Could the irresistible Jim Sawyer be the thief who had hacked into her computer?

"How did you know about my China report?" Dia insisted after jumping off the bench. Her tone had quickly turned from friendly to confrontational. "I didn't talk about China at all in my job seminar. In fact, now that I think of it, I don't remember seeing you there."

"Oh, I'm sure I've mixed up some reports," Jim calmly replied. Checking the wall clock, he added, "Gosh, I'm late for an appointment. Dia, it was really great to meet you. I'm sure I'll see you around." With that, Jim exited the gym and hurried down the street.

Smooth, thought Dia. That could be the sign of an honest man, or of a crook. She planned to keep her eyes on Jim Sawyer.

5. ZURICH

Gunter Brater had managed accounts at the Lagner Bank in Zurich, Switzerland, for over twenty years. Account #TG-64321 had received only deposits; a withdrawal had never been made. All the account's deposits were invested in U.S. Treasury securities.

One bone-chilling, but sunny day, Brater received a faxed message from the account's owner. The message contained four words: "Be prepared to liquidate."

Such transactions were not unheard of in Zurich. Founded in 15 BC as a Roman customs post, today Zurich is a bustling, modern city and one of the major financial capitals of the world. Some call it a "city of bankers in a country of banks." Much like cattle being traded in Omaha or stocks in New York, people trade currencies of different countries in Zurich.

Currency trading may sound odd at first, but it's really straightforward. Investors trade currencies because they can make money doing so. Say, for example, two British pounds trade for one U.S. dollar (insiders would say the exchange rate for pounds and dollars is two to one). If investors, for some reason, thought the dollar would "strengthen" against the pound, this might mean it would take three pounds to equal one dollar sometime in the future (the exchange rate would then be three to one). Investors, especially those in Britain, would do well to buy dollars today—at the rate of two pounds for one dollar—and sell them in the future when they would get three pounds back for every dollar. In terms of British pounds, the investor would have earned a 50 percent rate of return. Not too shabby!

And what might make dollars increase in value against pounds? Well, many things, including better investment returns in the U.S. relative to Britain or faster printing of pounds in Britain compared to dollars in the U.S. International investors constantly speculate about movements in exchange rates, trying to guess where they can make the biggest investment killing.

Zurich is popular with the international money crowd for another reason—it's the home of the famous Swiss bank account. Want to hide money from your spouse, children, relatives, people who may sue you, or the government? The answer is easy—open a Swiss bank account. These accounts are identified by numbers, not names, and Swiss laws make it a crime for a banker to release any information about a customer's account. The accounts aren't cheap; most require an initial deposit of at least $100,000. But deposed dictators and divorced moguls who forgot prenuptial agreements have been able to maintain lives of comfort and style, thanks to Swiss bank accounts covering their paper trails.

Swiss bank accounts can be invested in anything. For investors who want to invest in a country's currency, the accounts often won't hold dollars, pounds, francs, or yen. Instead they'll hold bonds denominated in that country's currency. In this case the investor gets the benefits of movements in the exchange rate—if they're guessed correctly—plus the interest paid on the bond. For investors who want to hold U.S. dollars, the most popular investment would be Treasury securities issued by the U.S. government.

And that's what Gunter's client was preparing to liquidate.

6. SHOT DOWN

Adam Kasten stormed into her office without knocking. His face was flushed all the way up to his rapidly receding hairline, giving him the look of a newborn infant squalling to be fed. He slammed the report on Dia's desk. She stared at him, unable to guess what had her boss so upset.

"This is totally unacceptable," spit Kasten.

"What do you mean?" Dia stammered.

"For starters, you write like you're continuing your dissertation." Kasten could barely get the words out before his eyes turned up to look at the ceiling. Dia thought she could see him mouth the numbers as he counted to ten so he could continue a bit more calmly. He took a deep breath, then resumed. "Remember you're presenting options to policymakers, not other economists. For example, listen to this:

> The current business cycle has now been in an expansionary phase for nine months. Real GDP is increasing, but at a modest 2.5 percent annualized rate, and a recessionary gap, while smaller, still remains. Although the unemployment rate has increased, most of the increase is structural or based on the return to the labor force of discouraged workers. The cyclical component has stabilized, and cyclical unemployment will begin falling as workers and businesses adjust to lower inflationary expectations. The Phillips Curve should shift downward, pushing the economy to a natural unemployment rate of 4.5 percent."

"But sir, these are standard macroeconomic concepts." Feeling unfairly attacked, especially after having spent so much time on the report, Dia responded more assertively than she otherwise might. Her superior now had his back to her, appearing to be mesmerized by some fascinating street scene observable from the office window. Not being able to see his reaction to her last statement was actually beneficial for Dia. It gave her the nerve to continue her defense.

"Everyone knows the economy goes through ups and downs, which we call the business cycle. The economy, in terms of its production of goods and services, is growing during an expansion and declining while in recession. Even newspapers quote real GDP, which is just the quantity of goods and services produced in the economy."

She watched as Kasten turned back from the window to face her. It was a relief to see his complexion had returned to a more normal color. Unlike Bowman, who maintained an impeccable style for his many public appearances, Kasten worked largely in the background, and he looked it. Short, with a middle-aged paunch under a rumpled shirt, a double-verging-on-triple chin, and only a little salt-and-pepper hair remaining, Adam Kasten looked a decade older than his actual midthirties. He was always on call to Bowman, and it wasn't unusual for him to log more than seventy hours of work a week, as the dark patches under his eyes revealed.

Kasten said nothing, so Dia forged ahead. "Recently the country was in a recession, meaning the country produced less than its potential—technically economists call this a recessionary gap. But since the economy has been growing, the recessionary gap is getting smaller."

"I admit I remember some of these ideas from my Harvard days." Kasten stopped pacing the narrow space between Dia's desk and her crowded bookcase and sat in an armless chair. "But Bowman won't have a clue. And what about this distinction between structural and cyclical unemployment? Plus, what in the world are discouraged workers and the natural unemployment rate? I'm sure someone who is unemployed won't say it's natural. Sounds like psycho-babble, not economics. Doesn't all unemployment still mean people don't have jobs?"

"Sure." Dia felt like she was teaching elementary macroeconomics again. "But the reasons for unemployment can be different, and these reasons are crucial for designing the right kinds of policies to address unemployment. Cyclical unemployment is the kind that increases during a recession. So since the economy is not in a recession, cyclical unemployment has declined."

Dia was standing and gesturing with her hands. Like her workouts at the gym, any physical movement had always helped her organize her thoughts and make her arguments more convincing during a stressful situation. "Structural unemployment is caused by big shifts in the economy," she continued. "The country is going through such shifts right now with technology and machinery replacing many manufacturing jobs. The displaced workers often don't have the background and training to go into fields that are adding workers, such as education, health care, computer science, and the professions."

"And discouraged workers?" Kasten pleaded, hopeful for a quick resolution to this detailed economic education he had unwittingly asked for.

"Discouraged workers are people who don't have a job and want to work, but they've unsuccessfully looked for work for so long that they eventually give up and stop sending out resumes and going to interviews," Dia politely responded.

"So what! They're still counted as unemployed, aren't they?"

"Actually not." Dia tried hard to suppress a smile. "According to the Labor Department's rules on counting unemployment, if a person hasn't actively looked for a job in the past month, that person is *not* counted as unemployed. I know this sounds silly, but the idea is to weed out those people who aren't serious about looking for work."

"So how can these people increase the unemployment rate? I would think they would cause the rate to go down." Kasten looked genuinely confused.

Dia was warming to the discussion now. Helping people understand core economic principles was as pleasurable to her as anything she could think of. "When the economy improves and businesses start adding jobs, discouraged workers will begin looking for work again. So they will again be counted as unemployed until they do find a job. That's why you can get the confusing situation of employment *and* the unemployment rate increasing at the same time."

"I see," Kasten muttered. Dia looked straight into Kasten's eyes, just as she did with her former students, trying to detect if he *really* did understand.

"Oh, I almost forgot," Dia excitedly said, as she was now in her "teaching zone." "The natural unemployment rate is just the rate that exists after cyclical unemployment has been eliminated. In other words, it's the unemployment rate that occurs when the economy has reached its full growth potential, and those people without work are either between jobs or are folks who don't have the skills and training needed to match up with available employment."

Dia paused and then asked, "Does all this help make sense of the report?"

Kasten was back up and pacing again. "It's cleared up some things, but you've really lost me with inflationary expectations and the Phillips Curve."

"I apologize. That is a bit of inside-economics jargon." Like most academicians, Dia knew economists could talk in their own brand of code. "The Phillips

Curve is based on the pessimistic idea that says the country can have high unemployment and low inflation, or low unemployment and high inflation, but it can't have both low unemployment and low inflation. Inflation, of course, measures how fast prices are rising."

Kasten stopped his pacing. He was now paying close attention to Dia's every word, because he could see this idea had big political ramifications.

Noticing his renewed interest, Dia took a big breath and plunged on: "The Phillips Curve really results from a mismatch between expected inflation and actual inflation. Let me put it another way. It takes time for businesses to realize the inflation rate has changed. Today, for example, actual inflation is falling, meaning prices are still rising yet at a slower rate that they did before. But businesses may still expect the prices they charge to be rising at the previous higher inflation rate. So they interpret a lower actual inflation rate as a decrease in purchasing from buyers, meaning their receipts are rising slower than their costs, and their profits are shrinking. This causes businesses to cut back by reducing the number of workers they hire. When this happens, you get the matchup of a lower actual inflation rate and a higher unemployment rate."

"This sounds hopeless," interjected Kasten.

"The story does end happily," Dia replied, trying to add some humor. "Once businesses come to expect the now-actual lower inflation rate, they won't see it as representing a decline in buying and a squeeze on their profits, so hiring will go back to where it was. As a result, over long periods of time the Phillips Curve really disappears, and the country can have lower inflation and lower unemployment together."

"So, like the old saying goes, hindsight is twenty-twenty." Kasten summarized Dia's detailed explanation with a cliché.

"Exactly, sir," Dia wasn't upset by his simple statement. She simply grinned pleasantly as she often did when a class full of economics students grasped her point. To her, it didn't matter how the concept was learned, as long as it *was* learned.

Kasten could tell he had more than met his intellectual match in Dia. Secretly the businessman in him admired her and wished he had her extensive training in economics. But annoyance replaced admiration with his next point: "Dr. Fenner, this next statement you make is appalling, and I quote:

> Our national economy is largely self-correcting. Indeed, any policies enacted
> to alter the business cycle can very well bring only temporary improvement
> and may ultimately slow the reallocations needed to return the economy to a

stable growth path. The key factors behind improving the nation's standard of living are building physical infrastructure, developing new technology, and upgrading human capital—i.e., the training of workers—not monetary or budgetary stimuli."

Kasten shook his head disgustedly and waved the report wildly about in his hands. "This sounds like a recommendation for doing nothing, which, Dr. Fenner, I can assure you will not be viewed kindly by the Secretary or, for that matter, by the President."

Dia was intelligent, and not just in her knowledge of economics. She could immediately see she hadn't considered the political overtones of her report. She had simply assumed her superiors would want only solid economic analysis. But Dia now viewed Kasten's questions as a challenge to her integrity, so with confidence rising anew, she ably countered his criticism.

"Assistant Secretary Kasten," Dia began. "I apologize if my writing has been too academic. The report represents my best thinking about macroeconomic policy, which was what I thought you wanted. There is a debate in my profession over the degree to which policy changes can have any lasting effects. Some economists believe the results may be temporary. For example, consumers may initially spend more money when tax rates are reduced, but the effects of the cuts wear off over time, especially if tax rates are expected to go back up. Another theory holds that the markets may anticipate impacts of the policy changes and therefore make those very changes ineffective."

Her boss had resumed his restless movements while Dia talked. Now he stopped and sat down. "Explain this further," he ordered. Kasten was listening intently. He recognized sound reasoning when it was presented, and he was eager to hear more.

"Well, say the Federal Reserve lowers interest rates to stimulate borrowing and spending. But what if the financial markets think the Fed's actions will increase the inflation rate as spending outpaces production? The higher inflation rate increases business costs, and the higher costs simply eat up the extra spending with no resulting change in production or employment."

"Hmm," Kasten pulled at his chin. He had cooled down again as he quickly concluded the implications of economic policies were more complex than he had thought. "Dr. Fenner, this is what I want you to do. First, rewrite this report." Here he paused dramatically, but with a hint of a smile. "Do it in English, so that the Secretary can understand it. Second, give us some real policy options that the Secretary can take to the President. Oh yes, and let's work hard to keep your opinions out of it."

"Yes sir, I'll get right on it." Dia was relieved the meeting was ending on a somewhat positive note, but she felt a little like a political hack for agreeing to muzzle her thoughts. She was quickly learning the government offices of Washington were much different than the classrooms of Cornell.

As Kasten was about to leave Dia's office, he hesitated at the door. His underling was obviously bright and well-trained in her field, but she had to rethink her approach in the politically charged Washington. Kasten looked back at Dia and said, "You've got a lot to learn about Washington, Dr. Fenner, if you want to be a success here."

It was as if Kasten had read her mind. Any sense of relief was gone. Dia felt depressed, thinking perhaps she had made the wrong career choice. Reluctantly Dia turned back to her computer. It would be hard to concentrate after her confrontation with Kasten, yet work had always been a way for her to deal with daily problems, inside or outside of economics.

This time it didn't help. Dia's depression immediately turned to fear as a message on her computer indicated the report she had submitted to Kasten had been copied by the hacker.

7. THE SUMMIT MEETING

Lawrence Bowman was in a foul mood as he was driven the few blocks from the Treasury Building to the corner of Constitution Avenue and Twentieth Street. Except for his frequent trips to the White House, he was used to people coming to see him, on *his* terms, and on *his* schedule. But today he was missing his regular squash game so he could play nice to someone who was his equal on the economic power chain, and someone from whom he needed a favor.

Harriet Hagerty was widely considered to be the most powerful woman in the country—maybe in the entire world. A wife, mother of three, grandmother of five, and former president of the American Credit Union, she now held the job that only fifteen people—all the rest male—had held in less than one hundred years: chairperson of the Federal Reserve System. She'd worked long and hard to assume such a powerful position in the male-dominated financial arena. Although she had the look of a grandmother in a Norman Rockwell painting, beneath the sweet exterior was a steely determination and iron will.

The Federal Reserve System, or Fed as it is commonly called, was established by Congress in 1913 as the nation's central bank. Although forms of a national banking system had existed since the 1800s, including a national currency, it became apparent the economy had become too complex and intertwined to continue without a strong central banking authority.

An important problem the Fed was created to address was the so-called "fractional reserve system." Banks originated simply as safe places for depositors to store money. However, eventually bankers realized not all those depositors came to claim their money at the same time. Being smart business people, bankers began to make loans based on those deposits and thereby earned interest on these loans. For example, if only 10 percent of deposits were needed on a given day to handle withdrawals by depositors, then the rest of the funds could be loaned. So, out of $1,000 in deposits, $100 would be kept in the vault and $900 would be loaned. Bankers had discovered the gold mine of credit!

This system worked fine as long as the economy was humming and people trusted banks. However, when the economy went sour, depositors would often worry and want their money out of the bank. If banks couldn't meet all the demands by depositors for withdrawals—which they usually couldn't—then "bank panics" set in. Banks would fail, people would lose their savings, and the economy would become that much worse. It could take years for the economy to revive and confidence in banks to be restored.

Several times in the nineteenth century wealthy individuals stepped in and loaned money to banks to meet the panics, but such bailouts couldn't be counted on all the time. What the country really needed was a bank of last resort—a sort of banker's bank—and this is exactly what the Federal Reserve is.

The Fed stands ready to make emergency loans to troubled banks. The Fed can arrange "shotgun weddings" between weak banks and healthy banks. The Fed also controls the fractional reserve system by regulating the percentage of deposits banks are required to keep in the vault for withdrawals.

But the greatest power of the Federal Reserve is its control over the nation's money supply. The Fed established a common currency in the nation called "Federal Reserve Notes." More significantly, the Fed controls the amount of this money in circulation, which today includes not only currency but also deposits at banks, such as checking accounts. If the Fed wants to increase the money supply, it purchases investments—specifically investments in U.S. government Treasury securities—from banks with new money. The new money then forms the basis for loans through the fractional reserve system. On the other hand, if the Fed wants to decrease the money supply, Treasury securities are sold to banks and money is withdrawn.

And where would the Fed get the money it used for these transactions, called "open market operations"? Literally out of thin air, or in today's more modern world of computers, by simply creating an electronic account!

Although open market operations are the Fed's most potent power, the Fed authority receiving the most publicity is its control over two interest rates. The discount rate is the interest rate charged by the Fed for loaning money to banks. So if the Fed wants to encourage banks to borrow money for its vaults and make more loans, the Fed will lower the discount rate. Conversely, if the Fed desires to discourage this activity, it will increase the discount rate. The Fed also directly controls another interest rate, the federal funds rate, which is the interest rate charged for money loans between banks. Usually the Fed will coordinate its tools, especially between the money supply and the federal funds rate. So an increase in the money supply and a lower federal funds rate will go hand in hand, just as a decrease in the money supply and a higher federal funds rate are dancing partners.

Harriet Hagerty didn't control the Fed single-handedly. A twelve-person "Federal Open Market Committee," composed of the Federal Reserve Board Governors—of which Hagerty was one—and presidents of regional Federal Reserve banks, met every six weeks to decide what dose of money the nation needed. However, the chairperson's control of the agenda and political clout meant she was rarely on the losing end of a vote. The last chairperson to face significant dissent within the committee, G. William Miller, lasted only seventeen months as head of the Fed.

Hagerty was not a member of the current President's political party. She had been appointed in the last year of the term of the President's predecessor. She had only one more year remaining on her four-year term, and she had made it known through political back-channels that she'd like to be reappointed.

Hagerty's opulent office in the Fed's headquarters within sight of the Washington Monument had the delicious smell of fresh brewing coffee. Hagerty had purposefully ordered the exact brand of coffee her next visitor liked. The meeting could go a long way in cementing Hagerty's chances for reappointment, and it had often been her experience that seemingly inconsequential details—like coffee preference—when noted and catered to, left a positive memory and appreciation toward the party involved.

A discreet buzz on her office phone alerted Hagerty the guest had arrived. Striding to the mirror to check that the lines of her business suit were still smooth, Hagerty briefly patted her short, silvery locks to ensure exact placement. Satisfied, she walked swiftly to the door. Her hand was outstretched as the door opened and the visitor entered.

"Larry, it's great to see you again," Hagerty said warmly as Lawrence Bowman walked in. "It's been far too long. I so enjoyed that party you and Margaret gave last fall, and we really should make it a point to get together again, soon."

Bowman returned the handshake and smiled: "Always a pleasure, Harriet. Thanks for seeing me on short notice. And by the way, the President sends his regards."

The Fed was viewed as a nonpartisan body. There were many instances of Fed chairs of one political party effectively working with presidents of the other party.

Republican Alan Greenspan working with Democrat Bill Clinton, and reappointed by Clinton twice, was the best recent example. Hagerty hoped to follow in Greenspan's footsteps.

"Harriet, I know you're well aware of the economic problems facing our country. The President thinks the time has come for a coordinated economic policy between the administration and the Fed," Bowman said, in between savoring sips of coffee. "We'll work on getting a tax cut and more federal spending. The President hoped that you and the Federal Reserve would see that the economic condition of the country warranted lower interest rates."

Bowman was referring to the two arms of national economic policy. The administration, together with Congress, operated fiscal policy. This policy involved changing taxes and government spending to influence the economy. The Fed controlled monetary policy, which had to do with the complementary changing of the money supply and short-term interest rates.

Hagerty smiled shrewdly. She knew she had an advantage here over Bowman and the President. Any fiscal policy proposals the President made had to be approved by Congress. This was no easy task, even if the President's party controlled Congress. Endless debates, committee hearings, parliamentary procedures, and sheer egos could drag out the discussion of the President's proposals for months, maybe even more than a year. John Kennedy's tax cuts designed to fight the recession he inherited in 1961 weren't enacted until 1964. And by the time poor Gerry Ford's proposals were finally implemented in 1975, the recession they were developed to end was over!

"Larry, I agree 100 percent" Hagerty said as she stood to refill Bowman's coffee cup. "I think I have enough influence over the Federal Open Market Committee to assure you approval of an expansion of the money supply and a reduction of interest rates at our next meeting in a couple of days." Hagerty was happy to remind Bowman of the speed with which the Fed could move and, more importantly, of her clout within the Fed.

"Well, that's great, Harriet. I can only hope the administration will be able to pull Congress along that fast." Bowman hated to concede this point to Hagerty. If only the pompous personalities in Congress wouldn't get in the way, things could move along equally fast in his arena. "What I wanted to do today was to set the groundwork and make sure we were on the same wavelength."

"That's fine, Larry, I totally understand." Hagerty was already thinking the meeting had gone very well for her. As she stood to face Bowman, she added, "Please tell the President I'm on board for developing and implementing an agenda to put this country back on track." Hagerty was glad she could subtly remind Bowman of the need for her cooperation. "And please say hello to Margaret again. We will just have to get together, soon."

Bowman clearly understood all that had transpired, both politically and economically. He managed a nod, one last sip of coffee, and a final handshake before he headed to the door. He too had accomplished his objective, but hated dealing with someone who had more cards to play than he. Unfortunately, that summed up all too well the power held by Harriet Hagerty, present queen of the Federal Reserve.

As Bowman left, he made one final comment, "Oh, Harriet, great coffee!"

Hagerty's smile faded as the heavy door clicked softly shut. She paused to stare at the lovely coffee set, rubbing her fingers thoughtfully along the rim of the server as she made mental notes. Point one: the meeting had definitely gone the way she wanted. But point two: had Bowman gained ground as well, small though it might be, in that annoyingly simple comment about the coffee? Somehow, he made her feel like a husband-serving female from the fifties. Was he that skillful in personal negotiations, or was he just being plain charming? Hagerty realized she'd have to give this more thought.

8. DATE WITH THE ENEMY?

Dia had been working nonstop since arriving in Washington. Here it was, a Saturday, and she had spent all morning in her cramped, cluttered office busily revising the report for Kasten. Although determined to do well in her new job, Dia had her limits.

The phone rang. Funny, she thought, no one knows I'm here at work. Somewhat annoyed to be interrupted and expecting a telemarketer or wrong number, Dia grabbed the phone and answered shortly: "Hello."

"Dia, hi, this is Jim Sawyer. I thought I might catch you there. It's such a nice day. What if I play tour guide and show you some of the sights of Washington?"

Dia didn't answer right away. To be honest, she was attracted to Jim and could really use a friend in Washington. She'd been so busy, she hadn't had time to meet many other people. But after her disastrous ending with Kyle, she was cautious. Plus, she couldn't quite decide if Jim was friend or foe. Was he the one who had been hacking into her files?

Dia decided to take a chance. "Sure, that's a great idea. Let me finish up a few things here, and we'll get together in, say, an hour."

"Super! I'll meet you across the street at the Old Ebbitt Grill, and we'll start with lunch." Jim couldn't have sounded nicer.

"It's a date," Dia said and hung up the phone. Wondering if she'd made the right decision, she glanced at her watch. She'd better get back to work if she wanted to finish the revision and be at the restaurant on time.

The Old Ebbitt Grill was a Washington landmark. Directly across Fifteenth Street from the Treasury Building and adjacent to the historic Willard Hotel, it was a popular gathering place for movers and shakers in Washington, both in and out of government. The setting was elegant and intimate, and the food was superb.

Normally the small lobby was crowded with people eager to be seated, but Saturday lunch was a slow time. It was her first time here, and Dia was impressed. Lights shone on rich, dark wood and brass banisters. Beautiful patterned ceramic tile at the entry directed patrons toward the short set of stairs leading to comfortable cozy dining booths and tables. Dia and Jim were quickly shown to a table. A waiter materialized out of nowhere to hand them enormous menus, quietly disappearing again to retrieve drinks.

After ordering, the pair settled into easy conversation.

"So, how do you like Washington so far?" Jim started.

Dia paused as the waiter returned to place glasses of wine on the table. "I'll admit I found it overwhelming at first, but I'm slowly getting used to it," Dia responded after taking a sip of her white wine. "How long have you been at Treasury?"

"Oh, not long." Jim seemed evasive and was quick to change the subject. "D.C. can almost eat you up initially, but you soon master it and love the opportunities that are here." He went on to discuss his favorite attractions—the Spy Museum, the newly opened American Indian Museum at the Smithsonian, and the outdoor FDR Memorial.

As Jim talked, Dia tried to get a read on him. He seemed to have no ulterior motive other than being a friendly colleague turned host.

After more chitchat about D.C. and family backgrounds, Jim suddenly turned the conversation to work. "Have you fully settled in to your office, or are you spending all your time on the Bowman project?" he asked.

The wine and excellent crab cake sandwich had relaxed Dia into feeling more at ease with Jim. Normally she wasn't one to make "much ado about nothing," but her emotional breakup with Kyle and the quirky happenings since her arrival in Washington had left her unsure. Even though it had been a less than stellar beginning to her new life in the city, she was determined to turn those experiences around.

"Yes, the policy paper has been taking all my time. I haven't even had time to read the personnel manual!" Dia looked at Jim with her right eyebrow raised to make sure he knew the last comment was meant to be funny, and he had. "Now I'm struggling with how to communicate the limits of macroeconomic policy in today's world to policymakers who expect quick results."

Jim leaned forward, giving her his complete attention. "What do you mean?"

Dia was glad to unburden herself about the problems she was having in making economic theory understandable to noneconomists. "Well, at the beginning of the twentieth century, most governments in leading countries had a hands-off policy to the macroeconomy. The assumption was economies would correct themselves, and intervention by the government would just delay these necessary corrections."

"You mean laissez-faire, or let the free market work?" Jim interjected.

"Exactly," Dia continued. "But this attitude turned around 180 degrees during the Great Depression of the 1930s. An English economist named Keynes developed a set of policy strategies governments could use to be countercyclical, meaning they would go against the prevailing business cycle. So Keynes outlined what should be done to accelerate economic growth during a recession and to moderate growth in an expansion."

"If I remember correctly, I think the U.S. adopted those strategies during FDR's presidency with the New Deal," added Jim.

"To a degree, yes, especially with government spending. Interestingly, Roosevelt campaigned on balancing the budget." Dia's knowledge impressed Jim. "But the important thing is that since the 1930s, it has been expected the federal government will take an active role in managing the economy. This has been largely accepted by Democrats and Republicans alike, although each had their favorite policy tool.

Dia took another soothing swallow of wine. "In fact, there's the famous statement in 1971 by Richard Nixon, who began as an anti-New Dealer, saying, 'We are all Keynesians now.' He meant all politicians, of whatever party stripe, believed the government had a mandate to move the economy. For example, both Democrat Clinton and Republican Bush Jr. created stimulus packages when confronted with a sluggish economy."

"So what's the issue?" asked Jim. "Isn't it expected the federal government will try to nudge the economy one way or the other? In fact, doesn't the average person expect the government to do just that?"

"Yes, but here's the problem." Dia was really enjoying both the academic discussion and Jim's company. "Many macroeconomists, myself included, have doubts about whether the government's tools can really work. Take the policy of cutting taxes to stimulate consumer spending. If the tax cut is temporary, studies show consumers will save most of the cut rather than spend it. That's because consumers tend to base spending on their permanent, long-run income, which a temporary tax cut doesn't change. Or if the cut is permanent but the government has to borrow money to finance the cut, this may reduce the lending that's available to consumers and businesses. Consequently, borrowing and spending by consumers and businesses will fall and simply offset the effects of the tax cut."

"Isn't that called 'crowding out?'" Jim asked.

"Why, it is," laughed Dia. Feigning a jab at Jim with her fork, she teasingly accused, "You know more macroeconomics than you've let on."

He looked pleased with the compliment. "So the idea of 'pump-priming,' where the government cuts taxes, increases spending, or does both to boost the economy during a recession, may just result in a couple of drips," Jim summed up. He loved word play, and the use of drips with pump-priming was just too much fun to resist.

"You're exactly on target—that's the heart of intensive debate right now in macroeconomics," she said. "But don't get me wrong. If the government could finance lower taxes by cutting out wasteful or unneeded government spending, then that would help the economy." Dia's enjoyment was obvious as she finished the last delectable bite of her crab. It was so satisfying to be able to mesh great food with intelligent conversation.

"But good luck having Congress decide what's wasteful and unneeded," Jim said as he rolled his eyes.

"You are so right," replied Dia, remembering from her public policy course the old adage that the only things with infinite lives were dirt and government programs.

The wonderful food, stimulating talk with an attractive man, and fabulous surroundings put Dia in a mellow, reflective mood. "Admittedly, Jim, there are some subtle points about the economy that matter a lot to economists but usually cause other people's eyes to glaze over. For instance, much of the discussion about the effectiveness of macroeconomic policy hinges on whether wages can freely change, or if they can't because they're restricted by contracts."

Jim listened intently, apparently impressed by Dia's knowledge and her ease in expressing it. "Give me an example," he prompted.

"OK, let's say the economy is in a recession. One of the usual consequences of a recession is that prices begin rising more slowly, or they may even drop. If workers quickly perceive this, they'll be willing to accept more modest wages and salaries, and this won't hurt them, because the purchasing power of their dollars has improved. As a result, businesses increase hiring, and the recession eventually ends without government action. In fact, in this case, government action may even work against this adjustment and delay it. The Nobel Prize-winning economist Milton Friedman thinks much of government macroeconomic policy is actually counterproductive."

"But the question is whether we live in this kind of economic world," Jim astutely added.

"Right again; you *are* good!" Dia replied playfully. "If we don't live in this kind of economic world, then some macroeconomists say this can serve as the basis for government intervention in stimulating the economy when it's in a recession."

Their conversation paused as the waiter brought another round of drinks and the dessert cart. Dia was delighted to see so many choices on it—how could she go wrong when they had three types of chocolate dishes alone? She allowed herself to go off her usually careful diet when she ate out. Dessert held no interest for Jim. Dia admired his willpower, misguided as it was in the case of dessert, in her opinion.

After the waiter left, Jim restarted their discussion. "Here's a question I have for you. How do you answer these radio talk show hosts who claim cutting taxes can bring in more revenue to the government by creating faster growth in the economy? In other words, they argue the tax cut can make the economic pie bigger, so much so that tax revenues are larger, even with lower tax rates."

Dia wondered if she really should have that second glass of wine with dessert, but she figured all the walking this afternoon visiting monuments and museums would wear off some of the effects of overindulgence.

"Sounds appealing, and there's a grain of truth to it, but as with most things in economics, reality is much more complicated. It's one of the mantle pieces of people who call themselves 'supply-siders,' although there's a lot more to supply-side economics than just tax cuts. Anyway, here's the issue in a nutshell." Before continuing, Dia gave the waiter a smile like he was Santa Claus as he placed the decadent looking white chocolate mousse cake in front of her. Just in case Jim changed his mind, she had ordered two forks.

"It's really a matter of arithmetic. Lower tax rates can cause the economy and tax base to grow faster, unless spending on important public functions like roads, education, and police and fire protection are likewise reduced. But there's no certainty a larger tax base together with a lower tax rate will produce more tax revenue than a smaller tax base matched with a higher tax rate."

"But are there any 'rules of thumb' that can tell us when lowering tax rates can increase tax revenues?" Jim queried as he waved off an offer of cake.

Dia looked thoughtfully at him. "You certainly are perceptive, Mr. Sawyer. Yes, the important cutoff seems to be 50 percent, especially for taxes on people's incomes. Lowering tax rates that are above 50 percent seems to produce more revenue, while reducing rates that already are under 50 percent doesn't."

With a wink of his eye, Jim said: "Dr. Fenner, I was really setting you up in a way. I already knew the answer you'd give me, because I read it in an article you coauthored with your major professor in the *Review of American Public Policy*. I think your explanation here was even better."

Suddenly Dia wanted to run out of the restaurant away from Jim. Her world once again seemed to be closing in on her. Indeed, she had addressed the question of lower tax rates providing more tax revenues. But it wasn't in the journal Jim mentioned—that article had been about monetary policy. Instead, she had just written the comments about tax rates this morning—in her office, in the revision to her report. Of this she was certain: only the computer spy would know that!

9. RESPITE

Reaching home as fast as the D.C. traffic would allow, Dia dove onto her sofa. She had muttered a hurried excuse to Jim about feeling sick from too much wine and the rich dessert and literally ran out of the restaurant. Her head was throbbing slightly from the wine, but what hurt more was her concern about Jim. All signs pointed to him being the hacker, but why? What could possibly be his motivation? Was it just a prank—was Jim hacking into Dia's computer because he could? Was it a form of stalking? Should she just go ahead and confront him?

Thinking about these questions only made Dia's head hurt worse. Seeking a diversion, she clicked on the TV.

"And today's guests are Lawrence Bowman, the Secretary of the Treasury and the President's chief economic spokesman, and Senator Edmund Trachsel, chairman of the Senate Finance Committee and one of the President's main critics. Welcome."

The guests smiled and nodded directly into the camera. They both knew how to play the media game.

The introductions had been made by Sherwood Ritman, a perfectly coiffed news anchor on the SBS network. The program, *Face the Issues*, was one of many virtually indistinguishable "talking heads" debate formats popular with cable channels.

It would indeed be a good diversion from her troubles—and, if she was lucky, make her forget her now splitting headache.

"Gentlemen, let me open by thanking you for coming," Ritman intoned seriously. "This week the latest national employment numbers were released, and the results appear to give us a mixed message about the labor market."

"Secretary Bowman, let me start with you. How do you read these numbers—good, bad, or uncertain?"

Dia had read the report and was keenly interested in Bowman's answer.

"Sherwood, the President pays close attention to the job market and is committed to increasing the number of good-paying jobs for Americans," Bowman stated firmly. OK, so much for the obvious. It was amazing how politicians could give responses without ever really answering the questions they were asked. What was even more amazing to Dia was the fact that newscasters usually let them get away with it. She turned her attention back to what Bowman was saying.

"And the President will not be satisfied until everyone who wants to work can work and can have a job that provides them with a decent standard of living."

"But Mr. Secretary, if I may interrupt a moment," Ritman said, "as I look at this new report on jobs, I see manufacturing jobs down, and although total jobs were up last month, the new positions were all in the service sector. Plus, since the President took office, the country has lost over a million payroll jobs." Ritman looked expectantly at Bowman, happy that he had put the Secretary on the spot.

Dia sat up a little straighter, her headache and recent troubles momentarily forgotten.

"Well, ah...Sherwood..." Dia was surprised to see the normally poised Bowman stutter. "Total jobs held by Americans are up by over two million since the President's term began. And as far as salaries are concerned..."

"Excuse me, but let me cut in here, Sherwood," Trachsel simply spoke over Bowman, a tactic that seemed to be a prerequisite for being a guest on these types of shows and one that the distinguished-looking, silver-haired senator had perfected. "I don't know what numbers my good friend Larry Bowman has been looking at—maybe he needs to get some new economists," chuckled Trachsel, "but when I see factory jobs going down and the unemployment rate going up, I know the American economy, indeed, the American family, is in trouble. Unfortunately, I don't see the administration doing anything to reverse these trends."

Annoyance was overtaking Dia's headache pain. She cringed at Trachsel's comment about economists.

"And one more thing, Sherwood, and I'm somewhat reluctant to say this..." Trachsel looked apologetic with his hands outstretched, palms up. "But it seems like in the past couple of decades, every time the President's party is in power, the economy goes into a recession."

"What about Senator Trachsel's points, Secretary Bowman?" Ritman asked with "gotcha" enthusiasm.

"Again, Sherwood, and Senator Trachsel, the President is committed to good jobs for Americans, and we've seen jobs increase…"

Dia didn't wait to hear the rest of Bowman's answer. All traces of her headache were forgotten. She was so riled up she almost threw the clicker at the TV. There was an obvious answer to support the administration's position. Dia yelled at the screen, "Tell him the difference between the payroll job report and the household job report."

Dia was referring to the two job surveys done each month. One, the payroll survey, counts jobs at existing businesses; this is the one Trachsel used. The other counts jobs by going to people's homes and asking if they have a job. This is the household survey, and Bowman based his numbers on this report.

The two reports can give different job totals for two reasons. First, each report is based on a statistical sample. The sample, or total number of households interviewed, for the payroll survey is bigger. So on statistical grounds, it gets high marks.

But the household survey gets points because it captures more kinds of jobs. While the payroll survey only includes people working at businesses that have been in existence for several months, the household survey will catch workers in brand new businesses and self-employed workers. It is a more accurate assessment of the job market.

"And I take issue with Senator Trachsel's misguided statement that our administration somehow brought on the last recession." Dia tuned in just in time to hear Bowman's answer. "That's like saying his party always gets us into wars."

"Touché," Dia said out loud. "Good comeback, Larry." Of course, Dia would never call Bowman "Larry" to his face. But his quick retort made her feel much better.

Dia certainly didn't consider herself a politically partisan person. Quite the opposite—she prided herself on being an independent who carefully analyzed political candidates and their positions. She knew it was absolutely silly to think one party caused the economy to do well and the other party didn't.

In fact, Dia was suspicious of any candidate who automatically claimed that, if elected, he or she would create millions of jobs and boost workers' salaries. Government simply couldn't do that. Yes, government had important roles in the economy, in areas like national defense, public safety, transportation, education, and—often overlooked—the court system, but it was workers, inventors, risk takers, and the new technology and ideas they developed that really moved the economy.

Dia's thoughts turned back to the TV to hear Ritman ask Trachsel, "Senator, do you have any thoughts on how we can increase the number of jobs available for Americans?"

Trachsel was obviously pleased to answer him. "Yes, Sherwood, I'm glad you asked this question. Look, I'm just a humble country boy, but if we passed legislation reducing the workweek to, say, thirty-five hours from the present forty hours, there would be a need to hire more people to do the same work, and unemployment would go down. You understand, this is just a simple idea from a plainspeaking public servant." Trachsel had a smug look on his tanned face as the studio lights bounced off his Rolex watch.

Ritman turned to Bowman with glee in his eyes: "Senator Trachsel has just made a concrete proposal to address the nation's unemployment problem. Will the administration support it?"

Dia shook her head. It was clear Bowman had been set up.

"We certainly will not, because it's a bad idea." Bowman's eyes were ice cold and his jaw set. "I was in business long enough to know that if you pay a person the same for less work time, the cost of labor rises, and businesses will hire fewer, not more, workers. Plus, there are some fixed costs, like training, benefits, and record keeping for each worker that will increase labor costs even further if more individual workers are hired to do the same amount of work that fewer workers were doing before. So, I think Senator Trachsel's idea would have the exact opposite effect than he expects. Simply look at France, where this proposal has been implemented, to see what I mean. Unemployment rates there are sky high."

"Attaboy, Larry," Dia shouted as she jumped up from the couch and clapped her hands in approval. "I didn't know you had it in you. There's some analytical brain matter inside those thousand-dollar suits after all!"

It was obvious from his expression that Ritman didn't agree with Bowman, but instead of commenting, he said: "Gentleman, unfortunately we're out of time. Thank you so much for being here. Let me thank our viewers for watching, and I invite you to tune in next week for another exciting edition of *Face the Issues*."

Dia was pleased. Her headache was gone, she had all but forgotten her worries about Jim, and she felt reinvigorated about her job at Treasury. Maybe she would enjoy working for Lawrence Bowman after all.

Face the Issues always drew a large audience. Michael Narone also had watched, and he, too, was pleased.

10. DECEPTION

Jim Sawyer lived in a small, yet comfortable efficiency apartment in the Capitol Hill neighborhood of Washington. The six-hundred-square-foot unit consisted of only three rooms: a galley kitchen with a barstool pressed against the counter that served as a dining area, a bathroom with stall shower and no tub, plus a combination living room/bedroom with the requisite sleeper sofa. A small, twelve-inch TV rested on top of a dresser in the combination room, and a lonely chair was the one concession for guests that never came.

Jim's spartan living quarters partly reflected his bachelor status. He was rarely there, using the apartment mainly for sleeping, while eating most of his meals out at diners, coffee shops, and the standard fast-food mainstays.

Jim was also a man who frequently had to travel light and move fast on a moment's notice. He kept a leather valise packed with the essentials deemed necessary for living on the road. He had no pets and no plants. He preferred a residence with few possessions or responsibilities because he never knew when he might have to leave them behind.

Jim did, however, enjoy his apartment's location. He was on the edge of a revitalizing neighborhood that was still a bit rough, but this had the advantage of deterring visitors from appearing uninvited. For work purposes, the unit was conveniently close to the seats of political power at the Capitol, White House, and Treasury Department. As a bonus it was near RFK Stadium, home of the new Washington Nationals baseball team, and not far from the future home of the Nats on the banks of the Anacostia River. Jim's one passion away from work was Major League Baseball, and no one was happier when the former Montreal Expos moved to Washington in 2005. He only hoped this latest version of Washington's team would fare better than the previous two did. While the city was shelling out several hundred million dollars for the new ballpark, Jim knew that ultimately a team's popularity depended on its win-loss record. Ballparks could be brand new or decades old, but how the game was played was still the most important thing to fans.

He looked at his watch. It was time to make the call. Because the phone line was secure, Jim always made important phone calls from his apartment.

"Sawyer reporting as requested." Jim spoke professionally into the receiver cradled in his hand.

"What's your progress, Sawyer?" the voice at the other end of the line asked.

"As instructed, I've been monitoring the targeted policymakers and their subordinates. I've been able to collect information both directly and indirectly. Soon I will finish analyzing and summarizing this information, at which point my report will be sent to you via the normal channels."

"Fine, fine." The voice sounded pleased. "But send your report sooner rather than later. Action will likely be taken within days."

"Yes sir, I will." Jim resigned himself to another late night of work.

"Have your activities drawn any suspicion?"

"I don't think so. As usual, I've made every effort to be very careful," replied Jim.

There was momentary silence as Jim sensed exhaling on the other end of the line. "What do you mean you don't think so, Sawyer? It's absolutely vital that your cover be maintained." The voice revealed a certain tenseness compared to its former pleased tone. "If our acquisition of information is revealed, the entire operation could be in jeopardy."

Jim focused and picked his next words carefully. "Yes, certainly I understand that, and I assure you I'm taking all necessary precautions. However, I must admit that one of my sources is extremely bright and perceptive, and at a recent meeting she acted rather strangely. It could be nothing. It probably *is* nothing, but I'll try to find out."

"Did you say *she*?" queried the voice. "I trust this doesn't imply a nonprofessional relationship has developed between you and this source, Sawyer. You know our position on keeping work and personal life completely separate."

"Absolutely, sir. I know, and I *am* maintaining a professional relationship with this source," Jim quickly responded. "She means nothing to me personally. I've befriended her so I can get access to the information and to the decision-making process."

"Very well, Sawyer. See that your relationship stays that way. We'll be in contact." With a click, the phone line disconnected.

Jim walked over to the apartment's lone window and stood with his arm propped on its sill. Resting his chin on his hands, he stared unseeingly out at the endless stretch of the city lights. He felt terrible. It wasn't because he had several hours of work ahead of him. He thrived on work. Instead, it was because, for the first time in his professional career, he had lied to his superior.

11. BLOWUP

Dia felt a mixture of emotions—elation, pride, nervousness, and a certain amount of fear. She was exactly where she had dreamed of being and doing what she wanted, but she was nearly trembling as she sat down with Kasten and Bowman.

Dia had been summoned to the Secretary's office to answer any questions he might have about her revised report on policy options. Once Bowman and Kasten were happy with it, politicos and media experts would transform the recommendations into "talking points" for the Secretary and other administration supporters to use with the press and Congress.

"Dr. Fenner, I've read over your report and I think it can serve as the basis for an economic stimulus program," Bowman said confidently. Dia initially wondered how much of the report the Secretary really had read, or whether he had even gotten past the executive summary. But after his strong finish on *Face the Issues*, Dia was willing to give him the benefit of the doubt.

Kasten, who was there to support Bowman, had digested every word of Dia's report. He stepped in to make sure Bowman understood the most important points.

"Mr. Secretary, I agree Dr. Fenner has outlined a workable plan for the administration. She recommends a two-pronged, aggressive approach. First, an across-the-board temporary tax cut combined with new infrastructure spending on popular projects like roads, schools, and public buildings."

Dia shifted uneasily in her chair. This was certainly what she had written, but it was also just what her superiors had wanted her to say. She was uncomfortable, because she knew her mentors at Cornell would not have approved such a simple approach.

Kasten continued: "Second, the administration will encourage the Fed to dramatically drop interest rates two percentage points and increase the money banks have available to lend."

"I like it, and I'm sure the President will like it," Bowman said, clasping his hands and looking positively giddy. "The President's ratings should definitely rise. After all, what's better than cheaper credit, lower taxes, and more government spending on things people can see and touch?" Dia shifted again.

"Now Dr. Fenner, assuming we can get the Congress and the Fed to go along, how long will it take for this program to get significant results in the economy?" The plan was useless to Bowman unless it kicked in well before the election, so the administration could receive full credit for the economic turnaround.

Kasten looked directly at Dia, waiting for her answer.

"The traditional models assert tax cuts and additional government spending, once implemented, can almost immediately increase national income and reduce unemployment. Interest rate cuts take longer to work their way through the system, with the initial effects beginning in, maybe, six months."

"Excellent," nodded Bowman. That kind of time frame was definitely to his liking.

For a moment, no one talked.

"Well, I guess that's it, then," Bowman said. "Thank you, Dr. Fenner. Fine work; absolutely first rate." He smiled broadly at Dia.

"Excuse me, sir, but I must add something." Dia boldly jumped in before the Secretary could completely dismiss her.

Kasten shot her a stern look that left no doubt as to his disapproval. She glanced at him, and then quickly shifted her eyes back to Bowman.

"Yes, Dr. Fenner," Bowman politely said.

"Sir, I'd like to respectfully inform you that I did not include more recent thinking and findings by economists on the effectiveness of fiscal and monetary policies."

"Oh," offered Bowman with raised eyebrow, "and why not?"

Dia paused to collect her thoughts before answering. "Because this new work casts doubt on how much government can really do to impact the macroeconomy. Quite frankly, I was led to believe it would be better not to include such questions in this report." Dia shot a sideways glance at Kasten. His disapproval was palpable.

Kasten interrupted. "Dr. Fenner, I think we can spare the Secretary the details of internal squabbling among economists." Part of Kasten's job was being a gatekeeper of economic policy information flowing to Bowman. Kasten worked hard to let the "right" information go in while keeping the "wrong" information out.

"Actually, Adam, I'd like to hear what Dr. Fenner has to say," Bowman forcefully inserted. He had picked up on Kasten's negative body language toward Dia, and his intuition—always successful in business—told him to find out what this was all about. "Go on, Dr. Fenner," he encouraged.

Dia had to physically flex herself and take a deep breath like she did in the gym before beginning her next exercise. But she reminded herself that this was what she wanted to do—to influence decision makers who matter.

"Secretary Bowman, there are three issues that many believe can reduce the effectiveness of government macroeconomic policies and may actually render them ineffective."

Always one to gesture when she talked, Dia used her fingers to emphasize each point. "First, consumers may not do what we expect them to do when the government implements its policies. Consumers may save a tax cut, especially a temporary one, rather than spend it. Or, consumers may not borrow and spend when interest rates are lowered." She knew Kasten was trying to catch her eye, so she looked directly at Bowman and ignored Kasten's furious stare.

"Second, there may be counterbalancing forces that negate the policies. Tax cuts financed by borrowing may reduce business spending. Or, additional government spending may simply displace private spending."

Bowman clearly hadn't heard any of these arguments. It was rapidly becoming obvious to him that many variables affected the economy, and isolating any one of them for change may not have the desired effect.

Dia finished making her points while she still had the nerve. "Last, the market—that is, consumers, businesses, and investors—may anticipate long-run implications of the policies and, effectively, counteract them. So, if tax cuts today mean deficits and higher taxes later, the two will cancel out each other, and private spending won't increase. Likewise, if lower interest rates now cause higher inflation and thus higher interest rates later, the market may go ahead and push up inflation now and offset the lower rates."

Bowman was stunned; Kasten was internally fuming. The best Bowman could muster was, "Really? Economists actually believe all this?"

"Well, not all economists, and those who do don't necessarily think all these offsetting effects occur 100 percent of the time. For example, it's a safe bet the Fed can raise and lower interest rates, at least temporarily," Dia explained. "And

many economists think government intervention can bring a recessionary economy back to full employment faster than letting the market self-correct, although
these economists are quick to point out the cost of this might very well be higher
inflation."

Dia took a deep breath. She knew once she was on a roll about economics, she
could almost smother people with her passionate, nonstop talking.

A soft tap was heard on the door and Bowman's administrative assistant
entered. "Mr. Secretary, it's time for you and Mr. Kasten to leave for your
appointment at the White House."

Bowman and Kasten stood. "Thank you very much, Dr. Fenner," the Secretary of the Treasury said. Dia couldn't tell if he was impressed or angry.

Bowman left first. Kasten paused a moment at the door in order to allow his
boss to walk out of hearing range. He turned to Dia with narrowed eyes and in a
menacingly soft voice said: "Fenner, I warned you about understanding how
Washington works and changing your ideas to fit political reality. You obviously
didn't take seriously what I told you. Now here's another bit of advice to think
about: you just might want to reconsider your career track."

12. BOMBSHELL

Dia was fuming. She slammed her office door, stormed the few feet to her desk, and threw herself down in the chair. She was so upset she could barely insert the key into her locked desk drawer. After several tries, she jerked it open. Grabbing her purse and slapping it open, she dug around until she found her cell phone. She punched a few numbers, seeking instant comfort.

"I blew it, Mom," she said, as soon as she heard her mother's voice. "I let my ego get the best of me. The Secretary liked my report. Why didn't I stop while I was ahead? Instead, I had to show them how much I knew and point out all the possible pitfalls of macroeconomic policies. I'm not cut out for this kind of government job. I should have taken a teaching position in a nice, quiet, college town."

Dia's mom, Ava Fenner, had an independent streak just like her daughter, and she believed wholeheartedly in her child. "Now you listen to me, young lady. You didn't spend all that time and money at Cornell, working part-time jobs and sacrificing so much of your personal life, only to become a 'yes' person," Ava said with conviction. Dia needed reassurance at this low point in her new career, and her mom was the one to give it. "Think about it this way," her mom continued. "It seems to me a responsible government would want you to tell them everything you know. As a taxpayer, I certainly do."

Just talking to her mother calmed Dia. "Thanks, Mom," Dia said with a more upbeat tone. "You'll never know just how much I needed to hear you say that. But there are some realities here that I'm just beginning to understand. My boss Adam Kasten warned me about understanding Washington. It isn't like graduate school where you're expected to question everything. I have to learn to keep my mouth shut and go with the flow."

"Well, that's just silly! Really almost dishonest," Ava snorted. "I have a notion to call my congressman and give him a piece of my mind about this Adam Kasten. Who does he think he is?" Ava was angry. She was protective of her "little girl," and like all mothers, would go to battle with anyone, anytime, anywhere when she felt her baby was being unfairly treated.

"No, no, no, don't do that, Mom." Dia protested. "I'll be OK, really, I'll be fine. I just needed to hear your voice. But I do have to go now. Talk to you again soon. Love you."

"I love you too, sweetie," Ava replied as she started to count. They had a ritual of counting to three before disconnecting. It was a silly game started long ago when neither wanted to be the first to hang up. Usually the ritual made Dia feel nostalgic, but not today. Her mind was too preoccupied.

Dia didn't know what to do next. She assumed Kasten would pay her a visit when he returned from the White House. Dia decided to see if she could add an appendix to her report where she "diplomatically" listed the reservations to standard fiscal and monetary policies.

Putting her phone and purse away, she turned to her computer and settled in to work. Dia kept FoxNews as her computer's home page. She noticed a just-posted headline flashing at the top of the screen: *Treasury Secretary and Fed Chief to Hold Joint News Conference at 2:00.*

Wow, an unprecedented conference. Never in history had these two powers held a joint meeting with the press. Normally the Federal Reserve chair liked to demonstrate the Fed's independence by not appearing too chummy with the administration.

Glancing at her watch, Dia saw it was a few minutes before two o'clock. She picked up the remote and switched on the small TV in her office.

Bowman and Hagerty stood behind matching lecterns, each embossed with their agency's official seal. The United States, Treasury Department, and Federal Reserve flags provided the backdrop. It was certainly impressive. The two looked like heads of state.

"Ladies and gentlemen," Bowman began, "Chairperson Hagerty and I have called this joint press conference to announce a coordinated effort to return economic growth and job creation to our economy. Based on careful and thorough work by both Treasury Department and Federal Reserve staff, we believe our plan, once implemented, will almost immediately restore confidence and prosperity to our country."

Dia flinched, knowing she was a big part of the staff.

"The cornerstones of the administration's plan are the tax cut and stimulus spending proposals, which we will submit to Congress immediately. We expect these to be considered and passed this week. Simultaneously, the Federal Reserve will lower its key interest rates by two percentage points and directly supply additional reserves to the nation's banks."

Bowman paused to let the statement sink in before adding, "Chairperson Hagerty, do you have anything to add?" Bowman made it clear who was running the show.

Dia saw how the pieces fit into place. Bowman and Kasten had known what they wanted all along. Her report had just been window dressing—sort of an academic stamp of approval—in case a reporter wanted background.

She turned back to the television as Hagerty announced the Fed would meet the next morning to vote on the interest rate cut and additional money supply. Hagerty said she fully expected an affirmative vote.

Bowman and Hagerty left the stage and were replaced by their press secretaries. Questions were hurled at them by reporters, but no new substance was added to what Bowman and Hagerty had already stated. Dia wasn't thrilled when her name was given as one of the "expert staffers" from the Treasury Department. She wondered if she should prepare for any phone calls from reporters.

Dia switched off the TV and returned to her computer screen to see how the financial markets were reacting. Pleasant images floated in her head as she remembered the first time she heard an economics professor tell her the stock market was like an ongoing election. Investors registered their likes or dislikes of economic policies, as well as all other economic matters, through their buying and selling on Wall Street.

So far the major stock market indices were up. Maybe this plan would work.

Just then the "New Message" indicator popped up on Dia's screen. She clicked on "Get Mail." To her surprise—and concern—there was another message from Kyle. The day continued to spiral downward.

13. BIRTH OF MONEY

"Yeah...OK...uh-huh...You're kidding! That much?" Harry Rector shouted into the phone to the caller from the Federal Reserve's headquarters in Washington. "We haven't had that much activity since eighty-seven after the stock market crashed. I guess the big bosses know what they're doing. We're here to do what they say, not to question their moves, so when you give us the word, we'll get right on it. Yeah...uh-huh...sure. You too. Talk to you later, Lou."

"What was that all about?" Jessica Anson eagerly asked Harry. "Is it important? Do I get to see something really big happen?"

Jessica Anson was an intern at the New York Federal Reserve Bank, the most prominent of the Fed's branch banks and the bank that carried out the orders of the Board of Governors in Washington. Although Jessica was studying economics and finance at NYU, she was still learning the ropes at the Fed.

Harry Rector was a twenty-seven-year veteran of the New York Fed. He knew all the ropes and more. Harry had lived through the market crash of '87, the stock market bubble of the late '90s, and the day he would never forget: September 11, 2001. In each of these cases, the Fed had taken bold action which, some claimed, literally saved the economy.

In a couple of years Harry planned to retire and enjoy his government pension on the hobby farm he and his wife had purchased in the Hudson River valley. Now his job was to teach what he knew—especially what wasn't always taught in the textbooks—to potential successors like Jessica.

The two looked as different as the generations they represented. Harry wore a neatly pressed white shirt with plain tie, dress slacks, and black Oxford tie shoes.

Jessica had on a billowy skirt, peasant shirt, and sandals. Her one concession to formality was to cover her various pieces of "body art," as Harry had suggested.

"Yeah, kid, I'd call this big. That was Lou Dockins in D.C. He phones in the instructions on what the big bosses—er, I mean the Board of Governors—wants to do about monetary policy. And the inside word is they're about to open the money spigots full blast."

"So we're going to print a bunch of new money?" Jessica asked eagerly. "May I watch?"

Harry admired Jessica's excitement and energy. At his age, Harry felt two steps behind in the energy department whenever he was around one of the newcomers. "Sorry, it doesn't work that way. The Treasury Department's Bureau of Engraving and Printing actually prints the money. We just give them the reason to do it."

"Huh? I don't understand." Jessica wondered if she'd missed some crucial days in her money and banking class.

For a moment Harry was transported back almost thirty years to when he was a rookie at the New York Fed. An old curmudgeon named George Wooley had taken Harry under his wing and explained the money creation process. Now it was his turn to continue the circle of knowledge with Jessica.

"Here's what happens," he begins. "I'll call my contacts in the investment departments at the big private New York banks. I'll tell them the Fed is ready to buy some of their Treasury securities. After huddling with their managers, they'll call me back and tell me what they're willing to accept as payment. We then take the lowest offers."

"Why Treasury securities?" interrupted Jessica.

"First, because all banks keep them as part of their investment portfolio. Of course, Treasury securities are investments with the federal government, and they're considered very safe. Second, the Fed is allowed to hold Treasury securities as investments. They can't hold stocks and corporate bonds."

"But what if the banks won't sell the Treasury securities to the Fed? Then what does the Fed do?" Jessica asked as she took a sip from her ever-present water bottle.

Harry could see Jessica would learn fast. She had an inquisitive mind and wasn't afraid to ask questions. "Here's one of the ways the Fed is different from you and me. If banks hesitate at selling their Treasury securities, the Fed just increases the price they're willing to pay until the banks are willing to sell!"

"That's pretty neat," Jessica agreed, "but can't that bust the Fed's budget?"

"Well, that's another unique feature of the Federal Reserve," Harry explained. "They have no budget, at least for this. Or, another way of saying the same thing, they have no balance on their checkbook like you and I do. Even the federal government doesn't have this luxury. If Congress and the President spend more than the government takes in, they have to borrow the rest. Not so with the Fed."

"Awesome," Jessica said, her eyes wide.

Harry excused himself to make a couple of phone calls to Bank of America and Citibank. Jessica watched him talking. His seriousness was often punctuated by a couple of chuckles. Harry was professional about his job but, at the same time, could enjoy it. Jessica hoped the same would be true for her.

When Harry finished, Jessica hit him with another question. "OK, so the Fed buys Treasury securities from banks when it wants to increase the amount of money in the economy. But I still don't understand how this puts more dollars in people's hands."

Harry put down his coffee mug emblazoned with the Fed's logo. "It's actually pretty simple. The checks the Fed writes to the banks to pay for the Treasury securities are counted as reserves that the banks can use as the basis for loans. Sort of think of the Fed checks as gold, like back in the days when the country was on the gold standard. When the loans are made, checking accounts are created, and checks are written, and presto, we have new money. Of course, you know checks are a big part of the modern money supply. Also, the new spending will cause the Treasury Department to print some new dollars and mint more coins."

"So the Fed could make us all rich by just constantly creating more money!" Jessica said gleefully.

Harry could see a smile on Jessica's face, so he knew she was joking. But he called her bluff. "You're the econ major. You tell me why the Fed can't simply create prosperity with more and more money."

"OK. If the Fed creates too much money, and it's not backed by something real—and here I mean products and services that people buy—then the only thing that will change is prices, and they'll go up. That is, we'll have higher inflation. Every country that's tried to 'monetize' its way to prosperity has learned this the hard way. I remember reading about Germany after World War I. Their counterpart to our Fed was creating money right and left. But the only thing this created was galloping inflation. It got so bad that restaurants wouldn't post prices on their menus, because between the time someone sat down for a meal and then finished eating, the meal's price would have increased!"

"Bravo," Harry said as he applauded, which caused some heads to turn in the office. "Excellent answer, Professor Anson," he teased.

Jessica looked pleased by her mentor's praise. "Thanks, Harry. But I do see a possible flaw in the Fed's money creation process. For the system to work, people have to be willing to borrow. What if people don't want to borrow? What if banks can't make the new loans because they can't find borrowers? Then the new money wouldn't get created."

"Hmm, I've never seen that happen before." Harry looked perplexed.

"Wait, wait, it's coming back to me now." Jessica jumped out of her chair. "What did that econ professor call it? Oh yeah, I remember, the liquidity trap."

"The liquidity trap! That doesn't sound good." Harry held his coffee mug in midair.

Their roles were now reversed, with Jessica as teacher and Harry as student.

"Yep," Jessica continued, "the liquidity trap occurs when consumer confidence is so low and the economic outlook is so bad that banks can't give loans away. This was a problem during the depression of the 1930s and in Japan in the 1990s. So it didn't matter that the Fed flooded banks with new reserves for loans and interest rates plunged. People still wouldn't borrow. I remember my prof said it was like the Fed 'pushing on a string.' New loans just wouldn't happen."

Harry couldn't help but feel pride in his protégé. The Fed had done well in hiring Jessica.

The two were silent for a while, as Jessica took another sip of water and Harry another gulp of coffee. They gazed into space, satisfied with their conversation and its conclusions.

Jessica broke the silence. "You know what, Harry? It seems like this money creation process would be a lot easier if the Fed just dropped cash out of airplanes."

"Don't laugh, but I remember a famous economist once suggesting they do just that. Of course, then we'd be out of a job, unless, of course, we could fly the planes."

"Oh well," Jessica said, "it's probably better to keep the money creation process much more mysterious. Think of all the fighting that would erupt if money literally fell out of the sky."

"Right, kid. Now let's get ready to create some money."

"You know what, Harry?" Jessica asked as she tossed her empty water bottle into the recycling can. "This Fed job is so neat I might just get a new tattoo with the word 'Fed' in the middle of a dollar bill."

Harry rolled his eyes.

14. STRIKE OF THE PAPER TIGER

Michael Narone and Philip Casini watched the press conference from the comfort of identical leather club chairs. The richness of the wood-paneled den with its imported Brazilian hardwood and finely crafted, custom-made stone fireplace reflected their obvious appreciation for the finer things money could buy.

"The time has come," Narone said solemnly, as the conference concluded. "I'll make the call to Zurich today."

"Are you sure?" protested Casini. "Aren't there other ways we can strike back? This operation will cost us a fortune. But if we keep our funds in place, there's an excellent chance we could make a fortune." In the past, Casini's appeals to Narone's greed had often swayed his opinions. This time it didn't work.

"No, no." Narone's voice rose with slight annoyance. He got up from his chair and began to pace the room. Back and forth, back and forth he went, trying to burn off any anxiety over the daring plan he was about to set into motion. "We settled this months ago. This is the most effective and surprising way to strike. We'll catch them totally off guard. And now we have all the information we need to do just that."

Casini looked dismayed but nodded his reluctant agreement. Narone took hold of his colleague's shoulders and gave them a brotherly squeeze. Then, turning away and taking a sip of his drink, he added, "A paper tiger has always been considered an empty threat. But after next week, the world will know that our paper tiger has real teeth, and they are deadly."

Narone flipped open his cell phone and placed a call to Gunter Brater.

15. CHAOS

As expected, the Federal Open Market Committee met the morning after the joint conference by Bowman and Hagerty. Overwhelmingly, the committee voted to lower the two interest rates they controlled—the discount rate and the federal funds rate—by an unprecedented two percentage points. They also approved increasing the Fed's purchases of Treasury securities from banks. It was widely thought short-term interest rates in the economy would soon begin to drop.

Kasten met with Dia after the press conference but said nothing more about the meeting with Bowman and Dia's reservations about macroeconomic policy. Kasten gave Dia the task of preparing a report on policy options for dealing with international trade issues.

Although she suspected Kasten meant the trade task to be "busy work," Dia welcomed the job. She saw it as an opportunity to more fully develop her ideas about dealing with some of the negative effects of freer world trade. Changing the "rules of the game" in trade always creates winners and losers. For example, hundreds of thousands of U.S. textile and apparel workers lost their jobs as a result of NAFTA and GATT, yet U.S. consumers benefited from the resulting cheaper clothing prices. What the U.S. didn't have—and what Dia was interested in exploring—was a way of transferring some of the consumers' gained benefits to the displaced workers.

Dia had decided not to reply to Kyle's e-mail. This one had been less threatening, but Kyle still wanted to meet to talk about their future. She didn't think they had any future together to discuss. Besides, she rationalized, her life was too hectic. The last thing she needed was Kyle adding another layer of worry to the ones she already had. If he wanted to mess with her life, he'd just have to get in line! Dia's main focus right now was on keeping her job and improving her standing with Kasten and Bowman.

The phone rang. "Yes sir, I'll be right there," Dia responded. It was Kasten asking her to come to his office. Dia was puzzled. Kasten had sounded concerned and serious, which she expected, but his tone was conciliatory.

As Dia was shown into Kasten's office, she was surprised to see Bowman there too. Her heart sank. Maybe she had just imagined a conciliatory tone. Was she going to be reassigned, or, worse yet, fired?

"Dr. Fenner, please sit down," Kasten said graciously. "Have you been watching the market reaction to the Fed's announced rate cut?"

Bowman sat silently in a chair in the far corner, the fingers of one hand touching those of the other, tent-style, his face blank.

"Actually I haven't, sir. I've been making a preliminary outline of the trade report you requested." Dia wondered why Bowman looked so grave.

Kasten tilted a computer screen in Dia's direction. "The concern is there has been no market reaction," Kasten said as he pointed to the screen. "The Treasury bill rate is actually a little higher than it was yesterday. This makes no sense." The interest rate on U.S Treasury bills is one of the short-term rates that would be expected to fall following the cut in the Fed-controlled rates. Clearly, Kasten wanted to know what was happening.

Dia directed her attention to the screen, saw Kasten was right, and thought the reaction was very odd. Despite her reservations about the long-run effectiveness of monetary policy, it always worked initially. To lower interest rates, the Fed buys Treasury securities from banks. As in any economic market, additional buying, which economists refer to it as *increased demand*, drives up the price of whatever is being bought. In this case, the price of Treasury securities rises. But since Treasury securities pay a fixed interest payment amount each year, when their price rises, their effective interest rate (the interest payment divided by the price) falls. This is how the Fed makes interest rates fall, even more so than the direct cut in the two interest rates they control.

Bowman spoke for the first time. "Dr. Fenner, what is said in this room stays in this room, understand?"

Dia didn't know whether to be relieved or more concerned as Bowman entered into the conversation. "Certainly, sir," she agreed.

Bowman rose and looked out Kasten's window. It was a blustery day, cold and overcast. The weather seemed to reflect the prevailing mood of the people inside.

"Dr. Fenner, the Fed's policy is not working as we wanted—as we expected. The President and I, quite frankly, are looking like fools. And our allies on Capitol Hill tell us the impotency of the Fed's action is making it harder for us to sell our fiscal stimulus plan."

Dia wondered where Bowman was headed.

Bowman turned, looked directly at Dia, and said in an almost pleading tone, "You warned us these policies may not work. Is that what's going on?"

Dia almost felt sorry for Bowman. Here was a man who was used to implementing strategies to address specific problems and having those problems solved. He was told these were the tools to fix the economy, and now the economic engine wasn't responding. He was obviously out of his element.

Dia knew she was on the spot, but suddenly she felt in command of the situation. "No sir, what's happening now with interest rates is beyond anything I would expect. All standard economic models show monetary policy can change short-term interest rates, at least for an initial period."

"Any guesses then about what's happening to keep interest rates from falling?" Kasten interjected.

Dia paused a moment to gather her thoughts. "Well, the best explanation I can come up with is that someone, or some group, is flooding the market with Treasury securities to counteract the Fed's purchases," Dia replied. "But this isn't usual. Holders of existing Treasury securities make money when interest rates are lowered and the price, or value, of their securities rises. This would make a nice profit for those holders. So there would have to be some other motivation."

"Like what?" Bowman asked.

"Still sticking to economics, there could be two reasons. As I indicated in our earlier meeting," Dia said, casting a glance at Kasten, "there is the possibility that investors may worry the Fed's actions will eventually result in higher inflation. The Fed has to support the lower interest rates by effectively creating more money. And if the money supply grows faster than the production of our factories, offices, and farms, then prices will rise faster to soak up the extra dollars, meaning we'll have a higher inflation rate. The expectation of higher future inflation will make any investment measured in a fixed number of dollars, like Treasury securities, less valuable, and this could motivate some investors to sell them."

Bowman didn't appear to follow all of Dia's explanation, but Kasten had listened attentively. "How likely is this?" Kasten asked.

"In my opinion, not very." Dia quickly added, "Experience tells us the higher inflation rate, if it occurs, won't show up until one or two years down the road. So investors would still be better off keeping the Treasury securities today. Plus, forecasting future inflation rates is very tricky and uncertain. For instance, few economic forecasters predicted the very low inflation rates of the late 1990s. Forecasting is not an exact science."

Kasten appeared to digest this information and then asked, "Dr. Fenner, you mentioned two reasons. What's the second?"

"The second reason is similar, but it adds an international dimension," continued Dia. "Higher U.S. inflation will lower the value of the U.S. dollar against foreign currencies. If foreign investors in U.S. Treasury securities expect higher U.S. inflation following the Fed's action, they may be motivated to sell the Treasury securities and convert the dollars to another currency before the dollar depreciates. But once again, I wouldn't expect this action to be immediate."

Bowman moved across the room toward Dia. "Dr. Fenner, I admit I don't understand all these economic relationships." Dia found his honesty surprising, and for a man of his elevated position, quite refreshing. "But here's what I'd like you to do. Give this situation more thought—immediately please—and tell *me* what needs to be done to put the stimulus plan back on track. If there are any additional resources you need, just tell *me*. I'd like you to give this your highest priority and report directly to *me*."

Dia was astounded. Bowman was cutting Kasten out of the process. "Yes sir, I will," said Dia.

As Dia moved toward Kasten's door, Bowman added, "And Dr. Fenner, I'm sure I don't need to tell you that the future of this administration may be resting on your work."

Both Bowman and Kasten nodded encouragingly to her as she left.

Back at her desk, Dia felt almost felt on top of the world. The Treasury Secretary needed her expertise. The President's political future could depend on her work. Serious stuff for a novice government employee and a newly minted PhD.

A message blinked on Dia's computer screen telling her she had e-mail. She hoped it wasn't another message from Kyle. Things were turning in a more positive direction, and she wanted them to stay that way. Dia was brought crashing back to earth when she read: DIA—MEET ME IMMEDIATELY AT THE STARBUCKS AROUND THE CORNER. IT'S URGENT—MAYBE A MATTER OF LIFE OR DEATH JIM

16. EXECUTION

Things were also coming to a head across the Atlantic. Lagner Bank of Zurich account #TG-64321 had received only deposits in the ten years since it was opened. It had grown to become the largest account in Swiss bank history.

Yesterday the bank received orders to immediately begin selling the securities in the account and buying U.S. dollars. The selling was to proceed at the rate of $1 billion per hour until either the account was drained or new instructions were received.

Gunter Brater executed the order with typical Swiss efficiency. He didn't think about the reason for the sale or its possible implications. That was not his job.

17. A WARNING

Jim was waiting in line as Dia entered the Starbucks on Fourteenth Street, just a couple of blocks from the Treasury building. With head averted, she stood silently next to him as he gave the counterman their orders. After getting coffees, they settled into a table as far from the other customers as possible.

"Thanks for coming," Jim said, breaking the icy silence. He took one look at Dia's unsmiling face and knew he had to say more. "I really do apologize for being so dramatic in my e-mail. I'm sure I scared you."

"Well, you certainly *did*." Dia felt her anger rising. "How am I—how is anyone—going to react when they're told their life may be threatened?"

Dia was torn over Jim. She had been attracted to him since their first meeting at the gym. In the conversations they'd since had, he seemed sincere. On the other hand, all signs pointed to him as the hacker. So, despite her feelings, Dia wasn't sure she knew how to deal with Jim, or more importantly, if she trusted him.

His next words brought her attention back to the present. "That's just it—you may be in danger," Jim said in a low voice.

"What!" Dia's jaw dropped, and her coffee slopped over the rim as she slammed the cup down on the table.

"Listen, Dia, I like you—I really do," Jim went on earnestly. "But you're in the middle of something that's bigger than all of us. Something that could really threaten not only your job, but your life as well." He stared at Dia.

She wasn't sure if she believed him or not. For most people, this kind of drama occurred only in books and movies, never in real life. Jim was trying to convince Dia it was for real.

"Go on," Dia said, unable to hide her growing uneasiness.

Jim took a breath. "I think there may be two threats to you."

"Two threats!" Dia couldn't believe what she was hearing.

"The first threat is political," Jim continued. "You know a lot, Dia, about policy and about people. The administration has been embarrassed, and they're looking to you to save their butts."

"That just happened! How could you know?"

"Never mind that," Jim calmly sidestepped the question. "The important thing is that you're valuable for what you know. In Washington, knowledge is power. So you could be a target. People in the administration who want to move up, or people outside the administration who would not like it to continue into a second term, could use, or abuse you."

"I can take care of myself. I was around academic politics in graduate school." Dia was convinced Jim was overreacting.

Jim shook his head. "Look Dia, there's a big difference between university politics and Washington politics. University politics might result in a corner office with windows or a more convenient parking space. Washington politics can ruin your career for life, or worse, can simply ruin your life."

Dia stared at the man sitting across from her. "You mentioned two threats. What's the second one?"

"The second threat may be foreign." Jim reached for Dia's hand. "The foreign threat is not necessarily interested in ruining your career or ruining your life." He looked unblinkingly into Dia's eyes. "They may be more interested in *ending* your life. And Dia," Jim said as he continued to hold her hand, "I've come to like your life very much. Please, please, think about all I've told you." With that, Jim rose and dashed out of the shop.

18. SEEKING HELP

Dia felt like her life was coming apart. Thoughts whirled through her head, barely staying long enough to even begin to make sense. The meeting with Jim had left her alternately worried, then angry, and finally stunned and fearful. But could she really trust him? Maybe Jim had made up the possible threats to divert attention from him and whatever agenda he was pursuing.

Then there was the complete turnaround at her job. First she's a virtual outcast for frankly speaking her mind; then the Secretary of the Treasury practically begs her to help save the administration. What next?

Oh yes—Kyle. She had tried to put him out of her mind, but she couldn't. Would he just appear on her doorstep, still as angry as he was the day they parted? Maybe he was following her, or perhaps he was the hacker. Would Kyle follow through on his promise to ruin her life?

Finally, there was the puzzling economic mystery: why weren't interest rates falling like they should? In the past, Dia always relied on the economy making sense, even when the rest of her life didn't. Was this changing, too?

Life was complicated, and it appeared to be getting more so.

Dia needed a break to clear her mind. She needed reassurance from someone she admired and respected, and she knew just who to turn to. She made a call.

"Hello, Garrett Foster here. How may I help you?" the voice on the other end cheerfully answered.

Dia couldn't help but smile a little. Same old Professor Foster, whose door was always open so he could respond to any student's questions and concerns. He was as at home speaking to a hundred undergraduates in an introductory economics course as he was in a graduate research seminar. He was just one of those nice people you occasionally come across in life, devoted to his work and the community around him.

But like many academics, Foster had a comical idiosyncrasy. He had never been able to get used to bifocals. So, Foster always kept two pairs of glasses at the ready—one for reading and the other for distance. At the countless meetings in Foster's office reviewing chapters of her dissertation, Dia was amused watching him constantly interchange the glasses as he went from looking at pages on his desk to looking up at her. Now she longed for such an innocent diversion.

"Professor Foster, this is Dia Fenner. I hope I'm not disturbing you." Dia still couldn't bring herself to call him anything other than Professor Foster, although he had encouraged her to use less formality since she was awarded her PhD.

"Dia, it's so good to hear from you," he replied warmly. "Of course you're not disturbing me. I always have time for my best student in Macroeconomic Policy. Now tell me, how are things in Washington? At the very least, interesting, I trust?"

"To be honest, Professor Foster, it's been hectic. You heard about the joint press conference with the Treasury Secretary and chair of the Federal Reserve, and the Fed's subsequent decision to reduce their interest rates by two percentage points and pump more money into the economy?"

"Yes, yes, of course. That was quite dramatic and unprecedented. The Fed usually doesn't like to be center stage," Foster replied.

"Well, I'm kind of in the middle of this," Dia said.

Foster chuckled. "Congratulations."

Some of the tension dissolved as Dia laughed too, "Well, thank you, sir. And in one way, I am thrilled, because I'm at the center of policymaking. But now the Treasury Secretary wants me to give him answers as to why interest rates aren't responding as expected."

"Yes, I noticed that too, and it is confounding." Dia could imagine Foster pulling at his chin and looking up at the ceiling as he rocked back in his squeaky office chair, something he always did when deep in thought.

"Professor Foster, I wanted to run this explanation by you," Dia continued. "In addition to the Fed's actions, the administration is simultaneously pushing a tax cut and infrastructure spending package through Congress that will significantly widen the federal budget deficit."

"Ah, the old double-barreled shot of monetary policy and fiscal policy. The administration certainly is serious about trying to jump-start the economy," Foster said with a note of academic skepticism in his voice.

"Yes, they are, and I was wondering if the anticipated higher budget deficit could be leading to higher interest rates, which in turn would swamp the Fed's efforts to lower those rates. That is, could fiscal policy and monetary policy be working against each other?" Dia could imagine drawing her argument on Foster's blackboard.

"Excellent hypothesis, Dia." Dia had come a long way since she walked into Foster's office as a shy student five years earlier. "Of course, the conventional wisdom among the media and general populace is that larger budget deficits lead to higher interest rates."

"Professor Foster, even four hundred miles away I can tell by your tone that you don't agree with the conventional wisdom," Dia asserted.

"It's certainly easy to understand why people think bigger budget deficits lead to higher interest rates," Foster began. "The government borrows more to fund a larger deficit, and this additional borrowing increases the price of borrowing—the interest rate. Therefore, the more the government borrows, the higher the interest rate."

"But I know that is too simplistic," Dia replied. "Yet how do I explain it to noneconomists?"

"I would make three points," Foster responded in his reassuring way. "First, any borrowing has to be put in context. Let's try this. Use the example of a family borrowing $50,000. If the family earns $25,000 a year, a loan of $50,000 is high. But to a family earning $250,000, borrowing $50,000 is small potatoes. So the size of government borrowing always must be put in context to the size of the economy."

"OK, but during a recession, the economy is shrinking, so any new government borrowing will be like a family losing income and then taking out more loans. So how do I tell people this won't necessarily lead to higher interest rates?" Dia asked.

"Ah, good point, Dia, but here's where the analogy between an individual family and the macroeconomy breaks down. If, when the relative size of government borrowing increases, borrowing by businesses and households declines by a comparable amount, there's no impact on interest rates."

"But wouldn't borrowing by businesses and households drop because interest rates increased?" Dia asked.

"But there could be another reason," Foster countered. "What if businesses and households anticipate the government increasing taxes later to pay for the new debt? Remember how the administrations of the first George Bush and Bill Clinton increased taxes after the big deficits of the Reagan years? If families and companies feared that would happen again, they would want to reduce their borrowing so they could save for the higher taxes down the road."

Before Dia could respond, Foster plunged on with the energy and enthusiasm she had always admired. "And one more thing I'd emphasize, Dia. The good empirical studies that have looked at the relationship between budget deficits and interest rates have found none. They have simply not found that interest rates increase when budget deficits grow."

"Professor Foster, I knew I could count on you for great words of wisdom. I..." Dia's intercom buzzed, stopping her mid sentence.

"Professor Foster, could you excuse me for just a minute?" Dia was annoyed at the interruption. She knew Foster was a busy man and hated the idea of putting him on hold.

"Yes, of course, I'll wait," Foster politely answered.

"Yes," Dia spoke impatiently into the intercom.

"Dr. Fenner, you have a call," Dia's secretary said. Her voice relayed a sense of urgency, which Dia adroitly ignored.

"Take a number and tell them I'll call back," Dia curtly replied.

"Dr. Fenner, I think you should take this. It's someone *very* important," the secretary answered, drawing out "very" for emphasis.

"OK, just a second," Dia agreed. She punched the button holding the line with Foster and said apologetically, "Professor Foster, thanks so much for your help. I'm afraid I have to go now."

"That's all right, Dia," Foster replied. "It's been a real pleasure talking to you again. Good luck, and please call anytime."

Dia had a big grin on her face as she pushed the button for line two. It was reassuring to know that at least some people in her life were exactly who she had always thought they were.

"Hello, this is Dr. Fenner. How may I help you?"

"Dr. Fenner, please hold for Senator Trachsel."

19. FLIGHT

Edmund Trachsel was the chairman of the powerful Senate Finance Committee. The name was somewhat misleading, because the committee's scope encompassed the entire U.S. economy and any government action affecting the economy. No tax or spending bill made it to the President's desk without going through the Finance Committee and Edmund Trachsel. Even the chair of the Federal Reserve had to appear before the committee twice a year and politely endure its questions.

Like many senators, Trachsel had presidential ambitions, and those ambitions could be furthered by attacking the present administration.

Dia felt her stomach jump.

"Dr. Fenner, this is Edmund Trachsel. I trust you're having a good morning." Trachsel oozed political charm.

I was trying my best to, up until now, Dia thought to herself. But she managed to say, "Good morning, Senator. Yes, I'm fine. How are you?"

Trachsel ignored her question and got straight to the point. "Dr. Fenner, I suspect you're aware of what's going on—or maybe I should say—not going on in the financial markets regarding interest rates."

"Yes sir, I've been following it closely," Dia answered professionally.

"Darnedest thing I've ever seen in my twenty-two years in the Senate. I'm no economist, but I do know the Fed can move interest rates around when it wants to—at least it has in the past," Trachsel said.

Dia was silent. What was this leading to? Certainly Trachsel hadn't called her to chat about economics.

"Well, here's the reason I called," Trachsel continued. "My committee is holding emergency hearings on the Fed's actions and the response of the financial markets. I know you're an expert on these matters, so I want you to come and testify." As he spoke, Trachsel was admiring the breathtaking view he had of the Capitol grounds from the window of his inner office.

Dia didn't know what to say. Trachsel's tone made it clear that this was actually a directive, not a request she could choose to ignore. She wasn't sure about the protocol—whether she could testify without Bowman's permission. She also remembered Jim's warning that she might be a potential target in political gamesmanship.

Dia composed herself and, in her best diplomatic tone, answered: "Senator Trachsel, I'm flattered, but wouldn't you rather have Secretary Bowman testify?"

"Hell, Bowman doesn't know what's going on." Trachsel's voice turned less friendly. "Listen, I pay the salaries of all of you people over at Treasury." The Senate Finance Committee did, indeed, hold the purse strings of the Treasury Department's budget. His comment did not go unnoticed by Dia.

She thought quickly. "Senator Trachsel, I certainly respect your position. But I think I should at least inform Secretary Bowman and Assistant Secretary Kasten of your request. Doesn't that seem reasonable?"

Trachsel wasn't pleased. "I suppose if you must, then go ahead. But let me tell you this. I always get what I want. And I want you before my committee, and soon. My staff will be back in touch with you to make all the necessary arrangements."

Dia was about to respond when she heard an abrupt "click." Trachsel had hung up.

*   *   *   *

That afternoon Dia once again found herself in the Secretary of the Treasury's office with Bowman and Kasten. She was summoned immediately after informing Bowman's assistant of Trachsel's request.

Bowman paced back and forth, with barely controlled anger in his movements. "The old coot wants to embarrass the administration and the President," Bowman fumed. "I don't think Dr. Fenner should testify." Bowman was looking at Kasten, not at Dia.

"But he has the authority to call her," Kasten reminded him.

Bowman thought for a long moment. Looking at Dia, Bowman asked, "Dr. Fenner, have you taken any vacation since coming to Treasury?"

"No sir. I've only been here a couple of weeks." Dia was surprised by this turn in the conversation. Of all the questions she had anticipated, that was not one of them.

"Well, I suggest you take a couple of weeks off. I'll work out the details with personnel. After all, you've been working very hard. You deserve a break." Bowman sounded almost fatherly.

"Sir, that's very kind of you, but I'm still in the middle of the analysis you were anxious to have concerning the market's reaction to the Fed's policy move."

Bowman's fatherly tone disappeared abruptly. "Never mind the report. I want you to take some time off. I strongly advise you to find a place to unwind outside of Washington. And one more thing: don't tell us where you go and keep your cell phone off."

20. IN HIDING

Getting out of D.C. was just what Dia needed. She cracked the car window open to allow the breeze to clear her head.

Her decade-old Honda had seen better days. Dia planned to replace it as soon as she accumulated some savings. She'd toyed with the idea of buying one of the new fuel-efficient hybrids, but the price tag deterred her. As an economist, Dia knew many financial decisions revolved around the old adage, pay me now or pay me later. With hybrids, you'd pay more now but save on gas later, whereas with gas-powered vehicles, today's price was lower but tomorrow's gas costs would be higher. This was a classic economic tradeoff that Dia would have to analyze more closely when she had time.

Right now though, Dia felt like a new person as she sped along the open countryside of central Virginia. She gazed at the various ways humans had shaped the environment. Washington was surrounded by several rings of development. First were the densely developed inner suburbs of Fairfax and Prince George's counties. Next came the transforming outer suburbs. Here houses in freshly built subdivisions bumped up against wide-open pastures. It was in the outer suburbs farther from the city's core where the battles over "sprawl" versus "open space" were most intense. Middle-income homeowners wanted to live there because of the cheaper housing prices ("more house for your money," advertised real estate agents), yet they had to endure long commutes. Farmers were happy to sell their huge tracts of land for development and become instant millionaires. But groups of environmentalists, preservationists, and highbrow city dwellers wanted to keep that land out of the hands of builders. It was the old economic issue of externalities. When did one person's right to use a resource in the manner he saw fit impact upon others' enjoyment of that same resource?

Dia now entered the next ring. The highly coveted, aristocratic Virginia "horse country" was more than fifty miles from downtown Washington. She drove through gently rolling hills and open fields, dotted with stands of trees. Livestock grazed contentedly in the sunshine, and thoroughbred horses lingered within the confines of white split-rail fences that seemed to go on forever. The peaceful surroundings allowed Dia to forge the past few days and put her mind at ease.

Dia had decided to follow her mom's suggestion and visit her cousins Tina and Stan Beattie. She hadn't seen them in years. They were considerably older than Dia in their midfifties, semiretired and busy trying to get a small winery up and running. The wine industry was booming in Virginia, with scores of wineries opening each year to cater to the aging baby boomers' newfound interest in the grape. Many of these upstarts generated sales through on-site winery tours followed by Internet sales. For years, state laws dating from the 1930s prohibited direct sales of wine across state lines. Out-of-state wineries were required to sell their wine through stores within other states. Tina and Stan, along with other new wine entrepreneurs, fought those laws all the way to the U.S. Supreme Court. Dia wasn't surprised the court eventually struck down the laws as anti-competitive and a restraint of interstate commerce.

Tina and Stan's place was about two hours from Washington, outside the small town of Glen Cove. As Dia drove up the gravel driveway to the house, she could feel the last bit of tension drain from her body. The long driveway hid the house and vineyard buildings from view. Along either side of the entrance, neat rows of grapevines extended up until the hills they rested on crested to meet the sky.

Coming to a crunching halt, Dia's car was barely stopped before her cousins came hurrying out to greet her. Stan, trim and still with a full head of red hair, opened her door and reached in to help Dia out before she even had her seatbelt undone.

"Honey, it's great to see you," Tina said, who had added a few pounds to her short frame since moving to Virginia. "We're so glad you came." They engulfed Dia in bear hugs. "We were hoping you would come down, but we didn't expect you could get away from your job so soon," Tina added.

Dia didn't want to go into the details on the circumstances of her "vacation," so she simply said, "One of the perks of a federal government job is the generous time off."

"Stan, take Dia's bags to the guest room. Then we'll sit down to supper," Tina directed. Like Dia, Tina was originally from the Midwest and still used that region's term for the evening meal.

Dia hadn't eaten such a wonderful home-cooked meal since the last time she visited her mom in Chillicothe. Like her own mother, Dia's cousins had cooked enough to feed "an army." Virginia country ham, black-eyed peas, sweet potatoes, and, of course, a couple of glasses of Tina and Stan's own Chardonnay conjured up pleasant memories of home and family. As Stan poured her another glass of wine, Dia found herself thinking that life could be so good. She was enjoying the Chardonnay and was curious to learn more about her cousins' second careers.

"So, tell me about the wine business. Has it been hard getting started?" Dia asked.

Tina, who loved to talk and could easily monopolize a conversation, had just taken a mouthful of food, so Stan answered first. "It hasn't been a picnic. Many of our friends envied us and thought developing vineyards and making wine would be fun. But starting any new business is hard, and I think it's especially true for the wine business. After eight years we're just beginning to make some money. In the first few years, all we did was invest in the vines and pray for the early crops to be successful."

Tina chewed furiously and swallowed so she could jump in. "We couldn't have done it without the security of our pensions. Banks are very skeptical about making loans for new ventures, especially ones as competitive as vineyards. Now that we're established, the bankers will talk to us. But despite the trials and tribulations, we absolutely love it. Being outside every day, checking on the grapes' development, and, of course, talking with the tourists have been wonderful."

Stan nodded his agreement.

"Well, the U.S. wine industry has certainly expanded beyond California," Dia said. "I think I read where nearly all states now have wine-making companies. Are you planning to sell your wine in stores beyond Virginia, maybe in other countries?"

Tina, taking small bites of food so she could dominate the discussion, said, "I'll tell you, Dia, when Stan and I were working at Milicron, we probably had the same opinion as most other people: always buy American and keep foreign goods out. But as business people, we see the flip side. If America keeps foreign products out, foreigners will likely keep American goods out of their countries."

As Tina paused and took a breath, Stan added. "And many of those foreign countries are growing by leaps and bounds, so they represent big opportunities for us. We reach customers using the Internet and now have buyers in twelve other countries, including France! Can you imagine French people enjoying wines from our little vineyard?" Stan beamed with excitement at the thought of European connoisseurs choosing to drink his wines.

"That's wonderful," Dia exclaimed. "You know, the media stays focused on the negatives of international trade, in terms of foreign products pushing aside American products and taking U.S. jobs. But there's certainly the other side of American companies selling to foreign buyers and creating U.S. jobs."

"I'm ready for competition," Tina said. "We make an excellent product, if I do say so myself. Let foreign and U.S. companies do the best they can, and then let the consumer decide." Dia smiled as she wondered how Tina's ideas on trade would be viewed by Tina's former colleagues at Milicron.

It was time for dessert, and Tina and Stan insisted Dia relax outside on the deck while they cleared the table and served fresh apple pie with a special after-dinner wine that was served ice cold. The food was wonderful, but the view from the deck was spectacular. Dia stood at the railing, admiring the land. Acres of carefully tended vineyards stretched before her. The vines ran down the hill as far as Dia could see, and each stalk was meticulously examined and cared for at least twice a week.

As bites of the spicy-sweet apple pie melted in Dia's mouth, Stan took the opportunity to ask Dia a business question. "Dia, I need to pick your brain. Do you mind?"

"Of course not, Stan. What can I help you with?"

"Well, I heard the Fed announced a decision to lower interest rates. If this happens, it will certainly be good news for us as borrowers because all of our loans are short term and 2 percent less on the rate will save us a bunch of money. But…"

Tina couldn't stand to be quiet for too long, so she cut off Stan's question. "Here's what I don't like," she said. "When the interest rate on our loans goes down, the rate on our investments, like CDs, goes down too. I wish we had CD rates like back in the 1980s, when they were, what, 12, 13 percent?"

A born teacher, Dia jumped at the chance to educate her cousins on investment economics. "The reason the interest rate for borrowing and the rate for investments move together is they're really the same rate. Banks and other financial firms are just middlemen. The bank takes the investors' deposits and turns around and loans them to other people. So if the interest rate on investments is low, the rate on loans will be low."

"Then how's the bank making any money?" Stan asked.

"They make money from the spread," explained Dia, "which is just the difference between the interest rate charged to borrowers and the interest rate paid to depositors. But that spread will be tiny, in the tenths of a percentage point."

"Still, I wish we earned those big CD rates of the early 1980s," Tina said.

"Here's the thing, Tina." Dia got more comfortable, propping her feet on the deck railing. "What matters is not the stated interest rate you're paid, but the interest rate you're left with after subtracting the inflation rate, which measures how much dollars are declining in purchasing power. Say you earned 13 percent on a CD in 1981. The inflation rate then was around 11 percent, meaning you needed to earn 11 percent on your investments just to keep pace with rising prices. What you had left over—2 percent—economists call the 'real rate.'"

Pouring Dia some more wine, Tina answered, "I understand that. But what if I earned 13 percent on a CD with the inflation rate at only 3 percent? Then I'd be left with a fat real interest rate of 10 percent. That's what I'd want." Tina grinned, thinking she'd won the argument.

Dia burst her bubble. "But that's just it, you never would. For something like a CD, high interest rates are paid only when the inflation rate is high. If the inflation rate comes down, so too does the interest rate. There's almost a one-to-one correspondence between the two." Dia loved this verbal jousting match.

"Oh," Tina said with disappointment in her voice. "I guess the little guy and gal just can't win."

Dia laughed. "Well, I don't know about that, but what I would say is you can generally only earn a higher real interest rate by taking more risk—like you're doing here with the winery—and everything works out. A big reason why real CD interest rates are so low is CDs are very safe, because they carry federal insurance."

"Oh," Tina said again, nodding in agreement. This time she appeared to truly understand the economic concept Dia had worked to get across.

With Tina checkmated, Stan saw another chance to get back into the conversation. Having forgotten the first question he tried to ask, he forged ahead to another. "Dia, I've always had a question about how inflation is measured. When I hear the government say the inflation rate last year was 3 percent, does that mean the prices of everything I buy went up 3 percent? That doesn't seem possible."

"It's not," Dia agreed. "Any inflation measure—and there are several—is an average of individual price changes. You've heard of the old saying, 'no one is average?' Well, the stated inflation rate won't match up with the price changes that you or I or anyone observes. In the case of the retail-level inflation rate, the Consumer Price Index, the government bases it on the spending habits of a sample of households."

Tina recovered and spoke up. "Didn't I read where AARP—you know, the American Association of Retired Persons—has long been upset with the government's inflation rate, because they say it doesn't adequately represent items that the elderly buy, like prescription drugs, which are rising rapidly in price?"

"You're absolutely right," Dia said, grateful that she could agree with her host. "In fact, this is a perfect illustration of how the average inflation rate doesn't represent the actual experiences of every group. Indeed, this is a big issue for senior citizens, because Social Security payments are increased each year by the official inflation rate."

"Here's maybe the most important question of the evening." Stan winked at Tina because she knew what he was going to ask. "With the Fed pushing interest rates down, we'd love to convert many of our short-term loans to longer loans and lock in these low interest rates for a lengthy time. Do you think that's a good idea?"

Tina and Stan stared at Dia with laser intensity because this was a critical financial issue for them.

"Certainly you'd want to lock in a low long-term interest rate on your loans if you could. But the Fed doesn't directly control long-term interest rates. One important factor that affects long-term interest rates is forecasts about inflation. The higher the expected average future inflation rate, the more lenders will charge on long-term loans, because higher inflation reduces the purchasing power of future dollars."

"So we can't necessarily count on long-term rates going down?" Tina's eyebrows furrowed.

"No, in fact, there are many times when short- and long-term interest rates move in opposite directions," answered Dia.

Stan also looked confused. "But that doesn't make sense, does it?"

"Actually, it does," replied Dia, eager to explain more economics. "For example, if investors sense that the Fed pushing short-term interest rates down and creating more money will cause future inflation rates to go up, then long-term interest rates can rise while short-term interest rates are falling. Also the opposite can happen. If the Fed raises short-term rates, and this is interpreted as reducing future inflation, long-term rates can go down."

"Whew, this is complicated," Tina said. "I don't know how you can keep all this in your head."

"Well, I still don't know if I have it all straight," Dia said, always shy about accepting compliments. "But I will say it keeps economics interesting."

"All I can say is I'm sure glad we have you in the family," Stan added as he gave Dia a loving pat on the back.

For a while nothing Dia and her cousins were quiet as they pondered the evening's conversation and enjoyed the view and cool night air. With no city lights around, the stars looked brilliant, and farther down the hill a quarter-moon peaked between heavily branched trees. *This is truly heaven on earth*, Dia thought to herself. She felt so peaceful and contented. Unfortunately, it wouldn't last.

21. SETTING THE TRAP

Despite his twenty-five years in the Virginia State Police, with the last five as commander, Gerald Hendrickson never got used to being an early riser. His wife said he always needed at least two cups of coffee before he was even tolerable. Anyone who ever worked with him would be quick to agree.

Commander Hendrickson was just starting his second cup at Highway Patrol Headquarters in Richmond when his secretary buzzed him.

"Yeah," Hendrickson said with his usual guttural growl.

"Sir, Senator Trachsel in Washington is on the line. He insists on talking to you personally," responded the secretary timidly.

What in the world does Trachsel want? thought Hendrickson. Was one of his staffers ticketed for speeding, or worse, picked up for drunken driving? It was ironic. Politicians passed laws for the rest of us to obey, yet they often wanted the rules bent for themselves. Henderickson shook his head as he put his mug down on the cluttered desk.

"OK," Hendrickson reluctantly said, "patch him through."

"Commander Hendrickson, Edmund Trachsel here. May I talk with you about a matter of extreme national importance?" Trachsel was friendly, yet direct.

"We're here to serve, Senator." Hendrickson bit his tongue as he spoke the words.

"Commander, a staffer at the Treasury Department, Dr. Lydia Fenner, is missing. We have reason to believe she may be in your state."

"Missing?" Hendrickson was all business now. He sat up straighter and automatically reached for pen and paper to take down any information Trachsel could offer. "She's been reported missing? For how long, Senator?"

Trachsel hesitated slightly before answering. "Well, she hasn't actually been reported missing. Let's just say we can't find her, and she's needed here in Washington," the senator explained.

"Don't her superiors at Treasury know where she is?" Hendrickson was legitimately confused.

"They say she's on vacation, but they don't know where." Trachsel's tone had gotten tenser.

Hendrickson sensed something rotten. "Senator, with all due respect, I don't know what I can do or should do. If the individual is on an approved vacation which her bosses OK'd, then what's the issue?"

Trachsel shifted into blunt mode. "Look, Commander, my committee needs Dr. Fenner for some important testimony that affects the course of our nation's economy. We think she's in Virginia. I want you to find her. Get right on this—if you will." The last part was added almost as an afterthought, which annoyed the commander greatly.

Now Hendrickson was really suspicious of Trachsel's motives. He wanted to tell Trachsel to take a flying leap, but he couldn't. Instead, he politely replied, "All right, Senator, we'll keep an eye out for her. We'll contact the Washington authorities to get a description and license plate number."

"Never mind about that. We're faxing those to you even as we speak." The hum of an office fax machine led credence to the senator's words.

At this point Hendrickson was ready to say almost anything to placate Trachsel, just so he could hang up the phone and get back to his coffee. "That's fine, Senator, thank you. I'll distribute the information to our field staff."

Trachsel wasn't pleased. "Commander, I don't think you understand the urgency of this matter. I want the finding of Dr. Fenner to be your top priority."

Hendrickson was the one getting steamed now. Trachsel was crossing the line, even for a United States senator. "I'm afraid I can't do that, Senator. The Commonwealth's State Police has other pressing matters."

Trachsel lowered his voice and spoke very slowly, "Let me indicate the importance of this matter, Commander. The Virginia State Police has a multimillion dollar grant request before the U.S. Congress for an upgrade to its telecommunications equipment, correct?"

"That's right, Senator Trachsel." Hendrickson had worked hard on the proposal. He was pretty sure he knew where the conversation was going, and he didn't like it one bit.

"Let me make this really simple," Trachsel continued. "If I hear of the Virginia State Police apprehending anyone, and I mean anyone—escaped convict, hit-and-run driver, or chicken coop burglar—before Dr. Fenner is located, then you can kiss that telecommunications grant good-bye. Have I made myself clear?"

"Perfectly, Senator." Hendrickson was glad he had only three years left until retirement.

22. ROTARY

Scrambled eggs with chunks of spicy sausage accompanied by fresh fruit salad and piping hot coffee left her totally satisfied. After such a hearty country breakfast, Dia was grateful for the walking tour Tina and Stan gave her of the grounds and winery operations. She was impressed to see that Tina and Stan did everything "by the book" and used the very latest and best equipment.

Although machines were certainly important, the winery business remained very much a labor-intensive industry. Every season brought a new set of hands-on tasks. During the winter each plant was trimmed of its smaller branches to promote stronger growth, and the paths between the rows of vines were plowed to destroy the surface roots and force the plants to push stronger roots deeper into the soil. In spring the fields were cleared of debris, and branches were painstakingly threaded through horizontal lines of wire to support the emerging clumps of grapes. Low-lying clumps were cut and removed during the summer to allow the plant to devote its full resources to the premier grapes higher on the vine. Fall was the most hectic time. The grapes were carefully harvested by hand, the bad ones winnowed out, and the processing and aging begun. One of the perks was the constant smell of the grapes' rich fragrance.

Although Tina and Stan could do every one of these chores, they needed help to accomplish them on time. At twenty acres, their vineyard was relatively small, yet there were simply not enough hours in the day to attend to all the plants in the timely manner required. Like most vineyard managers, Tina and Stan hired hourly labor during peak times. Many of the seasonal workers were Hispanic and had little formal education. They migrated to the U.S. during the busy agricultural months and returned home in the slow months. Although the wages Tina and Stan paid the workers were not high by U.S. standards, they were by the standards of the migrants' home countries. So Tina and Stan got the labor they needed, and the workers improved their standard of living—a "win-win" for both parties.

Despite their hard work, Tina and Stan's success was subject to the whims of nature. Too much rainfall or not enough rainfall, or modest changes in the humidity could reduce an entire crop's quality and send the value of the resulting wine plummeting. Seeing their operation gave Dia a much better idea of the risks involved in being an entrepreneur.

Dia was impressed by Stan's running commentary on grape production methods as they made their way through the rows of luscious looking fruit. As they walked, Tina mentioned that today was their weekly Rotary luncheon. "Why don't you come along?" she asked Dia. "Everyone there is involved in business, so I'm sure they'd love to talk to you, I mean, you being an economist and all."

This was almost the last thing Dia wanted to do. She didn't feel like answering questions about the economy and government policy. But Tina was persistent. "Come on, Dia, it's not like you'll have to speak. We always have a scheduled speaker. You'll sit with Stan and me, get to meet some of our friends, and have lunch on us. We're meeting at one of our favorite restaurants, so I can guarantee you'll get a great meal."

OK, Tina and Stan are being nice enough to let me stay here, so I should try to please them, Dia said to herself. "Sure, that sounds like fun," Dia said, permitting herself a little lie.

The Glen Cove Rotary Club met in the cozy back room of the family owned Biscuit Basket Restaurant in the middle of town. As Dia entered, she thought back to her father attending Rotary meetings in Chillicothe when she was young. The oldest of service clubs in the country, the name was derived from the fact the weekly meetings initially rotated among the offices of members.

A voice boomed across the tables, cheerful and exuberant. "Tina and Stan, right on time as usual," bellowed Bob Powell, this year's president. Bob was a rotund, cheery man whose waistline matched his outgoing personality. He warmly shook Tina and Stan's hands as they entered the room. "And I see you've brought a guest! Great!"

"Bob, this is our cousin, Dr. Lydia Fenner. She's visiting us from Washington. Her father was a longtime Rotary member back in Ohio," Tina offered as she gave Bob a peck on the cheek. Before she knew what hit her, Bob enveloped Dia in a huge hug. Bob's enthusiasm for meet and greet was known throughout the small farming community, and today was no exception.

"Dr. Fenner, welcome," Bob said as he vigorously pumped Dia's hand. "Are you a physician or surgeon?"

"No, no, I'm not in that league." Dia thought she should be a little self-deprecating. "I'm a PhD type doctor, in economics."

"Well, that's still impressive. I know it took you years of study to get your doctorate. I'm so glad you could visit us," Bob said as he moved on to greet the next arrivals.

After Tina and Stan exchanged hellos with several other club members, they all went through the serving line. The Biscuit Basket was known for its large, homemade biscuits, and there was a stack of them just waiting to be consumed by the hungry Rotarians. Dia took one, along with a generous scoop of apple butter, and then moved on down the line to add samples of salad, green beans, and some kind of chicken. She grabbed an unsweetened ice tea, but skipped the banana pudding dessert, and then followed Tina and Stan to a table near the speaker's podium.

The meeting began with a brief welcome from Bob Powell, followed by the Pledge of Allegiance, and then settled in to contented chewing and polite chatter. Dia agreed, the highlight of the Biscuit Basket was indeed the biscuit with apple butter. She finished her salad and green beans, but after picking gamely at it, left most of the "mystery chicken" on her plate.

During the meal Tina and Stan introduced Dia to the other members at their table. Dia exchanged information about her hometown and her college years but purposefully left things vague about her Treasury job. She wanted to keep a low profile.

Promptly at 12:45 (Rotarians are known for their punctuality), President Powell called the meeting to order. Announcements were made about club members who had been recently admitted to or released from the hospital, followed by an update on club plans for a hot dog booth at the county fair. Visiting members from other clubs and guests were then recognized. Dia stood and gave a smile and a wave as Tina introduced her.

Following the routine details of the meeting, Bob Powell again took center stage at the podium. "Fellow Rotarians, as you know, we had a fine speaker lined up for today's meeting," he said so loudly that the microphone he was clutching seemed unnecessary. "We were going to hear from Pete Swindell on his project of placing purple martin houses in fields near the state forest off of Route 731. I know those of you who hike are excited, because these birds will help reduce the mosquito population. But Pete twisted his ankle yesterday and is in a lot of pain, so he couldn't be with us. Not to worry, though. I thought I'd entertain you with some stories from my days as a postal carrier."

There was a collective, good-natured groan from the audience.

"Wait a minute." Tina bounced up off her chair. "We've got someone right here who can give us a great talk." Tina looked directly at Dia. "My cousin Lydia is a high-level economist with the federal government. Everyone has questions about the economy. I'm sure Lydia can give us some answers. What do you say, Bob?"

Dia wanted to crawl under the table.

Before Bob could answer, there was a chorus of "yea, yea" from the group. Dia wondered if the response was as much in support of hearing her economic words of wisdom as it was a dismissal of Bob's postal day anecdotes. Bob waved a reluctant Dia to the podium. "Come on up here, little lady," he beamed broadly at Dia as she scraped her chair back and stood up.

"Thank you, thank you very much," stammered Dia. "I appreciate your interest in the economy. I obviously don't have any prepared remarks." She shot visual daggers at Tina as she spoke. "So maybe I'll let you just ask me questions, and I'll do my best to answer them."

Hands flew up as if Dia had asked who wanted to win a million dollars. Dia wished the undergraduates she had taught at Cornell had been this eager.

"Yes sir," Dia said pointing to a middle-aged man in casual attire.

"When are those people in Washington going to do something serious about the national debt? It doesn't seem like it matters what party is in control, we keep adding to that debt. I don't know how many trillions of dollars it is. Heck, if I ran my company like that, I wouldn't be in business long. I really feel sorry for my children and grandchildren. They'll have to bear the burden of all this borrowing. Shoot, if I were in Washington, I'd just cancel the debt. We owe it all to foreigners anyway."

"Thanks, John, I think we get your point." Bob had jumped in to pull John off his soapbox. "Let's give Dr. Fenner a chance to answer."

Dia took a deep breath. The national debt was always a hot-button issue, but there was also a lot of misinformation about it. "John, there are actually several questions in your comments, so let me see if I can address each one. First, your comment about foreigners owning all of the national debt. Foreigners actually own about 25 percent of the total national debt or 40 percent of a narrower measure of the debt. John, do you own some Treasury securities or U.S. savings bonds as part of your investments?" John nodded yes. "Well then, you own some of the national debt. I doubt you'd want the government to cancel the national debt, because if it did, those investments would be wiped out." John looked taken aback. He'd never thought of it that way.

Dia continued. "John, I take it from your comments that you think the government shouldn't have any debt."

"That's right, government should be run like a business," John said.

"But the fact is, most businesses do carry debt, and so do families," explained Dia. "And there are logical reasons for doing so. If a business or family is buying something that lasts a long time and provides benefits to them over that period of time, it makes economic sense to spread your payments over that same time period. And the way you do that is to borrow funds to purchase the asset, and then pay off the debt over time while you're using the asset. Think of how few families could own a home without taking out a mortgage, which is just a type of debt." John nodded his head, understanding her point once again.

A man in blue overalls broke in. "But the things that businesses and families go into debt to buy are valuable, like homes, cars, and tractors."

"That's an excellent point." Dia knew it was always good to compliment your audience. She remembered a TV talk show host in Ohio who always opened his show by telling his largely female audience they were the most beautiful group of women he had ever seen. He began hosting when she was a child, and the last she knew, was still going strong.

"Actually there are valuable assets the government buys where borrowing makes sense—roads, bridges, schools, military equipment, and the space shuttle, to name a few. What economists have long recommended is for the federal government to follow the lead of state and local governments and the private sector by setting up two budgets. One, the capital budget, would allow borrowing for long-lasting assets like I just mentioned. The second, the operating budget for day-to-day government functions, would have to be balanced."

Dia saw some nods of approval around the room. She looked around for another question and called on a petite woman in a business suit.

"I'm worried about our country losing good-paying jobs through outsourcing," the woman said. "I can understand sending low-paying jobs to other countries. But now I see high-paying computer and tech jobs being shipped overseas. I have a son completing a computer science degree at Virginia Tech. Will he have a job when he graduates?"

This was touchy question, and Dia knew she had to be careful with her answer. She understood the motivation of companies to seek the lowest cost inputs, and since computer science grads doing routine programming were available by the millions worldwide, it made sense that many of these positions would go overseas. However, this wouldn't satisfy someone who had a personal stake in the issue.

"Quite frankly, I can't guarantee your son will have a job when he graduates, and I know that's not what you want to hear. The economy has always changed, and it looks like the pace of change has quickened. With our economy becoming increasingly integrated with the world economy, there will be situations where U.S. companies put jobs in foreign countries. But don't forget that foreign companies are also creating jobs in the U.S. Look at all the foreign auto factories that have sprung up, as well as foreign-owned pharmaceutical plants. My recommendation for your son is for him to acquire training beyond a standard computer science degree that will make him more specialized and marketable and less likely to be replaced by a foreign worker."

A slightly built, scruffy-looking member yelled out the next question without raising his hand: "Wouldn't a lot of our economic problems be solved if we went back to the gold standard, where our money was backed by something real? Isn't our paper money essentially worthless?"

"Don't mind Jason—he's our resident complainer," someone shouted to a round of laughs and smiles. Even Jason laughed. The comment was apparently made with affection.

"Well, then why do you use the paper money if it's worthless?" Dia asked, looking directly at Jason.

"Because I have no choice," Jason answered. "Everyone uses our paper money."

"Ah-ha," Dia said in her best Sherlock Holmes imitation. "That's exactly the point. Everyone accepts our dollars and coins as payment. Paper money is a convenience, so we don't have to carry around items that are inherently valuable to use as payment. It also saves time compared to bartering, where you have to find someone who has something you want and in turn wants something you have. Using money, you only have to find someone who has something you desire."

Dia paused to appreciate the looks of understanding, which were perhaps the highest reward a teacher could receive. She continued, "People willingly use money as payment as long as it can't easily be counterfeited, and it holds its value for a reasonable time. But the bigger the economy and the more transactions that occur, the more money we need. That's a key problem with gold. Supplies are limited, so the amount of gold-backed money wouldn't necessarily keep up with our growing economy. Such a situation could lead to both falling prices and falling wages and salaries, something economists call deflation. The government does, however, need to watch how much money it prints. If it prints too much, money rapidly devalues, which is another way of saying we get a jump in the inflation rate."

"We have time for one more question," Bob interjected.

Dia called on an elderly man, who was dressed as a traditional Southern gentleman—navy blue suit, white dress shirt, blue and gray striped tie and wingtip shoes, with a hat plated carefully on the table near his plate. "Dr. Fenner, thank you so much for gracing us with your presence and sharing your considerable knowledge." Dia immediately liked this person. "When I was a young man, the economy around here was supported by the tobacco and textile industries. They gave employment and livelihood to thousands of people. Now those industries are dying a rapid death. What will replace them?"

The audience fell silent. Clearly this man held a position of respect in the club, and Dia could understand why.

"Sir, let me be honest," Dia began. "I don't know what exact jobs will be here in five, ten, or twenty years. I'm afraid people put too much faith in economists' ability to predict the future. By its nature, the economy is unpredictable, because no one knows with certainty what inventions, products, technologies, and business opportunities will be developed. That said, we do have some educated guesses. Jobs in education, health care, trades such as electricians and plumbers, transportation, management, and finance are expected to increase the most. And the majority of these jobs are decent paying if the person has the right training. But I can't guarantee the jobs will be here in Glen Cove. I'm sorry, but your children and grandchildren may have to move to get these jobs."

Before the club president could rise to thank Dia, the room burst into applause. Several members came up to Dia later to thank her or to ask other questions. Dia answered them all pleasantly and was surprised to find she enjoyed herself. Over in the corner, Tina and Stan glowed with pride.

23. CAUGHT

After returning to the winery from the Rotary meeting, Dia decided she needed some downtime away from her cousins. It was a warm day with a clear blue sky, perfect for some solitary solace in the car after her unexpected performance at Rotary. Dia had the CD player cranked up full blast with Barry Manilow's latest release, *Manilow Scores*. Listening unfortunately brought Kyle to mind. He had always threatened to chuck all her CDs out the car window, with, as he put it, "Manilow Snores" the first to go. The end of their relationship seemed much more obvious to Dia now. Even minor differences like their tastes in music had always been a battleground. She should have seen this, and other larger conflicts, ultimately cutting their bond.

She decided this forced vacation had been good for her. It was refreshing to renew acquaintances with her cousins. They had been nothing but gracious, and the winery would provide the ideal refuge when the pressures of Washington became too great. Even her reluctant front-stage performance at Rotary had ended up being surprisingly fun and rewarding.

Humming along to the music, she could feel herself mellowing out. Dia glanced at her gas gauge. It was under a quarter of a tank. She'd better fill up while it was on her mind.

Spotting a little country store at the intersection ahead, she turned in. The front windows of the small, white building were almost covered with artwork done by local schoolchildren. What a charming idea, Dia thought as she got out to gas up. The store had two sets of gas pumps, one facing the road Dia had been on, and the other facing the perpendicular road.

She chuckled as she looked at the gas prices. The media had been making a big deal about how gas prices were at an all-time high. To an economist, the price of any product must always be put in perspective of all other prices. A specific price is "higher" only if it has risen faster than other prices. Looked at this way, gas prices were not at a historic high—that dubious record still belonged to the early 1980s.

Returning the nozzle to the pump, Dia fit the gas cap on her car and went inside to pay. Many rural stores still didn't take credit cards at the pump.

"Hiya, hon," said the friendly middle-aged woman behind the counter. Dia smiled as she returned the greeting. The cashier was surrounded by the usual "impulse" purchases—candy, gum, cigarettes, magazines, and—because this was the South—NASCAR hats. Dia thought it amazing that she could now name five or six of the drivers. She was definitely not a racing fanatic, but you couldn't help remember the smiling faces and brightly colored uniforms you so often saw in advertisements and interviews.

Why not, Dia thought as she bought a Dale Earnhardt Jr. hat as a souvenir. Besides, she noted as she glimpsed herself and the cap in the mirror, the red color went well with her black hair.

Walking back to her car, Dia glanced to her right toward the other set of pumps. There stood Kyle filling the tank of his motorcycle. She was terrified. How could someone she had once loved so much now create the opposite emotion? And what was he doing *here*?

Their eyes met, and Dia could tell Kyle was surprised. He immediately replaced the nozzle and started toward her.

For a split second Dia felt she should stay and confront Kyle, but she quickly thought better of it. Kyle's threatening e-mail flashed in her mind, and she didn't know for certain how serious he had been or what he was capable of doing. Dia ran the short distance remaining to her car.

"Dia, wait, I need to talk to you," Kyle shouted.

Kyle's call was to no avail. Dia was already in her car and heading back to the highway. In her rearview mirror, Dia saw Kyle stop, turn around, and race back to his cycle. Was he about to chase her?

She didn't wait to find out as she pushed the speedometer well past sixty. She felt a twinge of panic. Could she remember how to get back to the winery? Suddenly all the country roads and turns looked alike.

"It doesn't matter. I've just got to put as much distance as I can between us." Dia often talked to herself when she was nervous. "Once I know Kyle is gone, I'll find a phone and call Tina and Stan for directions." Dia had been so eager to be alone for awhile that she had forgotten and left her cell phone at the winery.

Dia looked backward again and felt a stomach-wrenching adrenaline rush. Kyle was close behind her and appeared to be gaining fast.

Dia took a sharp right turn at the last possible moment, hoping to catch Kyle unaware and lose him. If she hadn't been so scared, Dia might have found humor in her driving style since donning the Earnhardt cap. The evasion didn't work. Kyle expertly maneuvered his cycle, leaning into the turn and continuing the pursuit.

Dia was taking some chances. She accelerated to seventy—much too fast for the two-lane road—and took many of the curves virtually on two wheels. Kyle effortlessly followed. Dia steadied herself. *I won't kill myself just to get away from him,* she thought. She slowed.

Now Kyle was only a few feet from her bumper. He was waving his left arm furiously and pointing for Dia to pull over.

Just then Dia heard a loud noise, like a roar from a large motor. There were no other vehicles in sight. Where was it coming from? Suddenly Dia realized the noise wasn't on the ground but came from above. She bent over the steering wheel and looked up as well as she could through the front windshield. Amazingly, a helicopter was hovering over her car!

When she looked forward again, she screamed. Not far ahead, the road was blocked by a car turned sideways. If Dia didn't immediately stop, she would crash or be forced off the road.

Desperately Dia pounded the brakes. Her car skidded and came to a screeching stop only a few feet from the waiting vehicle. Dia could clearly see the crest of the Virginia State Police on the side of the car.

The patrol car's passenger side door opened, and from it emerged a tall man dressed in a three-piece suit. He walked directly to Dia's car.

"Miss, are you Dr. Lydia Fenner?" the stranger asked as he showed Dia a badge. It was the badge of a U.S. Marshal.

"Yes, I am. What's this about? You know I could have been seriously hurt crashing into that car." Realizing what had almost happened, Dia was more angry than scared.

The marshal handed Dia an envelope. "Dr. Lydia Fenner, you've just been served by the United States Senate." The marshal calmly walked back to the patrol car, and it sped away.

Stunned, Dia turned around. Kyle was gone.

24. TAKEN

Dia had read the key words from the subpoena scores of times: "Dr. Lydia Fenner is called before the Senate Finance Committee." They sounded so plainly ominous. She was directed to appear Tuesday at 10:00 AM. A Senate limousine would be at her apartment at 9:00 AM to make sure she complied.

Dia didn't tell Tina and Stan about the subpoena, and she didn't mention Kyle. She simply told them she was sorry she had to leave so suddenly but had received word she needed to hurry back to Washington for an important meeting. As she hugged them good-bye, she promised to return soon for another vacation. She silently hoped the next one would end on a happier note.

Bowman and Kasten told Dia they weren't surprised at the subpoena. They knew she would eventually have to testify. But they had hoped to delay her testimony until after interest rates began falling. Unfortunately for them, rates still hadn't dropped.

Dia couldn't sleep. Giving up on getting any rest, she got up very early Tuesday morning. She was too nervous to eat much, so she had a light breakfast and then showered. Every one of the five suits she had bought for work was out of the closet and lying haphazardly all over the bed. She tried the burgundy suit on once again, turning this way and that in front of the mirror before deciding it would have to do. She could dress it up a bit with her grandmother's pearl necklace.

Dia stood at the window, holding the curtain back to glance anxiously up and down the street every few minutes. Finally, a black Lincoln Town Car pulled up to the curb in front of her building. She glanced at her watch. Nine o'clock. The limo was right on time. Dia had only ridden in a limousine once before—when her parents had rented one for her high school graduation. Getting inside, she discovered the Senate limo was even more plush, equipped with all the modern comforts and conveniences a top politician might want: bar, satellite TV with DVD player, several phones, laptop computer, and a combination fax and printer. Amazed by the opulence, Dia didn't dare touch anything. She just sat still and looked.

The drive downtown went smoothly considering the midmorning Washington traffic. It was probably just Dia's imagination that traffic lights turned green and vehicles moved over as the limo with U.S. Senate plates sped by. The car passed many landmarks—the National Portrait Gallery, MCI Center, FBI Building, and Union Station—all places Dia hoped to visit if calm ever returned to her life.

All too soon they arrived at their destination. The hearing was to be in the Dirksen Senate Office Building, one of four congressional office buildings constructed since World War II to accommodate the growing size and scope of Congress. The impressive seven-story, marble-faced building sat northeast of the Capitol on Constitution Avenue. It was connected to other congressional office buildings and to the Capitol by a subway system. As soon as she emerged from the limo, Dia was met by a Trachsel aide and taken to the committee hearing room on the fifth floor.

Congressional hearing rooms are structured in such a way as to leave no doubt who is in charge. Senators sit at a long, imposing table elevated several feet above the floor. Witnesses sit at a small table at floor level. Senators stare down at witnesses from their lofty perch. The symbolism can't be missed.

Dia was shown to her seat at the witness table and was surprised to find another person already there.

He stood to introduce himself. "Hi, I'm Peter Willoughby, the assistant counsel at Treasury," the young, bookish-looking person said. Although apparently a law school graduate, Willoughby could have passed for a high school student.

Dia shook Willoughby's outstretched hand. "Are you here to testify too?"

"No, I'm here to make sure the questions they ask you aren't out of line. Think of me as your protector." Dia wished he looked a bit more imposing.

She wondered if Willoughby was really here as Bowman and Kasten's eyes and ears. He certainly looked nonthreatening, but maybe that was the idea. "Well, I'm grateful for the help, but I don't think I need protecting. I'm just going to tell the truth."

"Of course, but there's the truth, and then there's *the* truth," grinned Willoughby. The freckles on his face made him appear even younger, and the glare from the overhead lights caused him to squint through oversized glasses. "From time to time I'll probably whisper some advice to you about how to phrase something, if you don't mind."

"Oh, but I *do* mind. I know what I did and didn't do, and you don't, so..."

Dia stopped abruptly as a Senate worker came over to test her microphone. Willoughby moved to his seat and busied himself with some papers from his briefcase. Dia decided to let the matter drop. She turned around to take in the rest of the room.

Dia was the only witness present. The observers' seats behind her were beginning to fill with a combination of press, lobbyists, and administration members. Scanning the faces, Dia's heart jumped when she caught a glimpse of Jim.

Time seemed to drag on as Dia tried to concentrate on possible questions she might be asked. It was a full twenty minutes before the doors in back of the Senators' table opened, and the committee members and their staffs spilled in. In the rush of suits moving to their designated places, Dia noticed Trachsel was the last to enter.

Senator Trachsel called the hearing to order. As soon as he began speaking, video and camera lights turned on full force and focused on Dia. She felt beads of sweat form on her forehead, from nerves or the hot camera lights, or both.

"Ladies and gentlemen, we face a grave crisis in our economy today," Trachsel stated, looking directly into the TV cameras and ignoring the audience. "Millions of our fellow citizens are needlessly out of work, while corporations destroy jobs through automation and outsourcing. For months I have begged the administration to act. Now when the administration finally announces a plan, it is effectively rejected by the financial markets and rendered impotent." Trachsel paused here for effect. He wanted to make sure his words had time to sink in to all who were listening.

"The purpose of this hearing is to document the steps that have led us to this situation and to ascertain if incompetence by administration officials has created the predicament." Clearly Trachsel was playing hardball.

"We have one witness this morning, Dr. Lydia Fenner. Dr. Fenner, please rise to be sworn in," Trachsel commanded.

Before Dia could rise, Willoughby jumped to his feet and yelled, "Objection!"

"Objection?" Trachsel responded with a false look of perplexity. Clearly Trachsel was ready for this.

"Yes, we object on the grounds the witness is here only to provide background information on the nature of the current economy, and any such information will necessarily be subjective, because it is based on the witness's personal evaluation," Willoughby eagerly offered.

"And you know for a fact that is all we will ask this witness to provide?" Trachsel calmly retorted.

"Well, what else could she provide?" Willoughby sounded genuinely confused.

"Why don't you let us decide that, Mr. Willoughby? Now please sit down quietly and let Dr. Fenner be sworn in." A red-faced Willoughby plopped back into his chair. He was clearly outmatched by Trachsel.

Dia stood with her right hand raised as a Senate clerk led her to say, "I, Lydia Louise Fenner, do solemnly swear that the testimony I am about to give is the truth, the whole truth, and nothing but the truth, so help me God."

"Dr. Fenner, please state your full name, occupation, and professional background for the record," Trachsel requested with a toothy grin barely suppressed.

"My name is Lydia Louise Fenner. I am the senior economist to the Assistant Secretary for economic policy at the U.S. Treasury Department. I hold a PhD in economics from Cornell University with a specialty in macroeconomic policy."

"Dr. Fenner, thank you for appearing before this committee on such short notice, although I must say we had a whale of a time finding you. Now, you weren't trying to hide from this committee, were you?" Trachsel guffawed as he turned to his colleagues, who also snickered.

"Objection, leading the witness," burst in Willoughby.

Trachsel's demeanor immediately turned sour. "Oh, do be still Mr. Willoughby. We're only having a light moment with Dr. Fenner." There were numerous laughs from the audience.

Feeling like a wounded schoolboy, Willoughby slumped in his chair.

"Of course not, Senator," Dia answered. "I was on vacation. Although I must say, I was surprised by the extravagant means you used to find me." Dia impressed herself at how assertive she sounded, but she didn't like having her integrity challenged. If Trachsel was going to sling mud, she'd throw it right back.

For a moment it looked like an annoyed Trachsel was ready to spar with Dia, but he let her comment go and moved on to the substance of the hearing. "Now Dr. Fenner, did you develop a policy paper recently for the Secretary of the Treasury on the options available for improving the economy?"

"Yes sir, I did," Dia quickly answered.

"Did this policy paper include any reservations, or cautions, about the policy options?" Trachsel looked directly at Dia.

"No sir," Dia answered.

"Did an earlier draft of the report include such reservations or cautions?" Trachsel asked as he looked intently at Dia over his half glasses.

Dia wondered how Trachsel knew this. Then she remembered Jim's warning about Washington politics. She thought hard about her answer before replying, but decided honesty was the best response.

"Yes sir, it did," Dia said.

"Dr. Fenner, were you then asked to remove those reservations and cautions from the final report?" Trachsel now reminded Dia of a prosecutor zeroing in on his witness.

"Yes sir."

"And who ordered you to do this, Dr. Fenner?"

Dia didn't hesitate. "Adam Kasten, the Assistant Secretary for economic policy."

Trachsel waited for the answer to be absorbed by the other Senators and the audience. Some newspaper reporters were scribbling her words down as quickly as they could, while others appeared to be more relaxed, letting modern conveniences record for them.

"Dr. Fenner, my next question is very important. Was there information in the part of the report you were ordered to delete by Mr. Kasten that would have predicted what's happening now in the financial markets?"

It suddenly dawned on Dia what Trachsel was doing. Trachsel wanted to prove a cover-up in the Treasury Department of information that could have anticipated the current problems with macroeconomic policy. Kasten was probably not Trachsel's target. The target was likely higher up—Bowman. And it wouldn't end there. Bowman's resignation would be a major embarrassment for the President.

Dia could feel all eyes trained on her like gun sights. So many people were anticipating her answer. Millions were watching if the television audience was included. One cable channel was televising the hearing live. Dia wondered if her mom was tuned in.

Nervously biting her lower lip, Dia scanned the senators' faces. Her answer was crucial to Trachsel's probe. The room was silent, everyone awaiting the witness's response.

Dia sat up straighter in her chair. Hands calmly folded in front of her belied the churning in her stomach. Next to her, even Willoughby had become a spectator in the drama.

"No, Senator Trachsel, there was *nothing* in the deleted section of my report that would have suggested the outcome we're currently seeing in the credit markets."

There was a murmur in the audience and quick looks among the senators. Dia's answer was obviously not what Trachsel expected.

"Are you sure? Remember, Dr. Fenner, you're under oath."

"Yes sir, Senator Trachsel. I know of no empirically tested macroeconomic model that would have predicted an immediate increase in short-term interest rates when the Federal Reserve was purchasing Treasury securities. Based on today's economic conditions, it's simply not economically rational for this to occur," Dia confidently replied.

Dia saw several reporters leave the committee room to file their stories. Her answer was the climax of the hearing. Trachsel's goal of toppling a top administration member had apparently crumbled. The tension began to drain out of her.

Trachsel wasn't ready to give up yet. "So, Dr. Fenner, you're saying under no circumstances could the Federal Reserve's moves to lower interest rates actually increase them?"

"First, Senator, you asked me what *I* had written in the deleted section, and I wrote nothing that would have predicted the scenario you described." (*Take that, you arrogant manipulator*, Dia wished she could say out loud.) Instead, she continued on. "But in terms of the economics, the Fed's purchasing of Treasury securities immediately leads to more loanable funds available to banks, and given the same initial demand for loans, the price of those loanable funds—the interest rate—will fall. Now, depending on how production in the economy responds relative to the increase in the money supply, there may ultimately be an increase in inflation and a rise in interest rates, but models show these effects, if they occur, happen months down the road."

Her response stopped Trachsel cold. This was not what he had expected to hear. Some of his Senate colleagues were fidgeting, a sure sign they were ready to bring the proceedings to an end.

Dia answered questions from several other senators, but her essential conclusion did not alter: the administration had not ignored any information that would have prevented the current economic crisis.

A disappointed Trachsel glumly dismissed Dia without even a thank-you. On the way out of the hearing room, several reporters cornered her to get taped comments and video for their evening news. Typical of the way the media liked to portray politics as conflict, Dia was treated as a "David" who had just slain a "Goliath" in the person of Trachsel. Some reporters implied she had put new life into an administration on the ropes. Dia was very much in the spotlight. She answered every question with such efficiency and confidence that it seemed she'd been working the press for years. Finally the reporters let her go.

She was glad the hearing was over. Her plan was to hail a nearby taxi and get back to her apartment as fast as possible. She looked forward to relaxing and decompressing in a long, hot soak in a bubble bath.

As she emerged from the Dirksen Building, Dia was somewhat surprised to still see the Senate limo, apparently waiting to take her home. *Well, that's one classy thing about Trachsel; at least he'd pay for her ride home*, thought Dia with a triumphant smile!

The driver opened the door for her. As Dia entered the backseat of the limo, she was startled to see Jim sitting to the far side of the backseat. The door to the car slammed shut. Before Dia could say or do anything, Jim slid over to her side and placed a dark hood over Dia's head!

25. FINAL FEAR

"Get it off me!" Dia screamed as loud as she could, but it did no good in the soundproof limo. Plus the darkened privacy glass allowed no one from the outside to see in. Jim secured a restraint across her arms so she couldn't reach the hood.

"Dia, please stay calm," Jim said soothingly. "You're not going to be hurt. Trust me."

"What do you want with me?" demanded Dia. When no answer was given she defiantly said, "I knew you were no good." Although she willed herself to appear outwardly strong and in control, secretly Dia had never been this frightened in her life. What was going on? This was like something from a scary movie, and she wasn't thrilled to be cast as the heroine in imminent danger.

Talking helped Dia focus. "I should have avoided you from the start—you with all your charm and good looks. What's wrong, Sawyer, you can't get dates the conventional way, so you have to kidnap your prey?" As soon as she said the words, Dia worried she may have crossed the line and needlessly antagonized her abductor.

Jim ignored her last comment. "Dia, I can't stand seeing you this way, but I have no choice," he said as he reached for her hand and gave it a reassuring squeeze. She immediately pulled it away.

Dia tried to calm down. She decided to stop protesting. It wasn't doing her any good, and Jim was answering none of her questions. Keeping her senses may very well be her only means of eventual escape.

Listening desperately for clues, she was disappointed she couldn't determine where the limo was going. Several turns were made, and at one point she thought they may have crossed the Potomac River.

They now rode silently. After about a half hour, Dia could sense the limo driving down a hill, or possibly some kind of ramp. At the bottom, it turned sharply before coming to a complete stop. She could feel Jim's weight on the car seat shift as he turned toward her.

"Dia, it won't be much longer," he said. "Please believe me." She could hear anguish in his voice, but she was still so confused about what had happened to her in the last few hours, she didn't say a word. The door opened, and Dia was led out of the limo by strong hands firmly clasped on her right arm. Almost immediately she felt another person—maybe Jim—controlling her left side. With the two strong individuals controlling her movements, there was no chance for Dia to escape. She shivered even though it was a warm day.

Dia's captors led her along what felt like a concrete floor. Suddenly they stopped. The whoosh of automatic doors sounded as they opened. Dia was moved two steps forward before she heard the "whoosh" one more time. Next came a jerking motion. Now she knew what was happening. They were in an elevator, and it was headed down.

The doors opened, and Dia was directed out of the elevator. Then, to her relief, the hood was removed.

Blinking several times to adjust to light again, Dia was amazed by what she saw. It was an enormous office space stuffed with computer terminals, TV monitors, and scores of people. The room buzzed with the sounds of fax machines, printers, and cell phones.

Jim looked straight into Dia's eyes. "Dia, I can explain now. This is FIFASA, the Federal International Financial Activity and Surveillance Agency. It's a highly sensitive part of the government, and this location is absolutely secret. That's why I couldn't allow you to see where we were going."

Dia momentarily forgot her anger. "So you're a spy?" she asked incredulously. "And I bet you're the one who has been hacking into my computer."

Evidently her first thoughts were pretty much on target. "I guess you could call me a spy—a financial spy," Jim answered. "FIFASA keeps track of large international financial movements. FIFASA's goal is to seize the funds of illegal organizations, especially drug rings and terrorists groups, when those funds come out of their hiding places onto the open market."

"And part of your job is to break into people's private computer files, even if those people are law-abiding citizens and government employees to boot, and kidnap them in broad daylight in front of Congress?" Dia asked, fire in her eyes.

"Yes, I did access files in your computer," Jim answered honestly, "and I apologize for doing that. But it's important for FIFASA to keep track of internal government policy discussions that might influence international financial movements. After all, the bad guys can get the same information from leaks and bribery."

"So Bowman and Kasten know who you are?" Dia wanted to know just how far this conspiracy went.

"Oh no, they know nothing about my real job. They honestly think I'm an international finance expert, which in a way I am. I have a master's degree in international economics from Penn. But, of course, I've had some specialized training beyond that."

"Like training in how to deceive people, snoop into their affairs, and hold them against their will." Dia's voice was sounding increasingly indignant.

"Look, Dia." Jim turned Dia around to face him. He was losing patience. "I'm sorry I misled you, and I'm sorry I invaded your privacy. But these are necessary evils in today's world. I still don't think you understand the important position you hold. You provide and receive all kinds of information, much of it capable of making great changes in economic policy decisions. In the eyes of the government, you're a bright and knowledgeable person…" His voice softened considerably. "And in my eyes too."

In spite of the circumstances, Dia was beginning to feel a little less hostile toward Jim. Almost surprising herself, her thoughts turned away from the current situation to how appealing Jim could be.

"I still don't understand. Why are you telling me all this, Jim? And why have you brought me here?" Dia's eyes searched his for answers, her anger dissipating.

"Two reasons." Jim said. "First, I wanted to protect you while FIFASA's operation was put in motion."

"Operation?" Dia looked confused.

"Yes, our operation to seize the account of one of the largest drug syndicates in the world, operated by Michael Narone and Philip Casini. These people are exceedingly dangerous, and they have operatives all over the world. Since you played an integral part in identifying them, I wanted you in a safe place when they realize what is happening."

Dia was spellbound. "What did I possibly have to do with identifying this drug ring?"

"Look up at the screen on the right. See the letters and numbers TG-64321. That's the number of a secret Swiss bank account worth billions of dollars and controlled by Narone and Casini. Now look."

Dia stared openmouthed as the word SEIZED flashed next to the account.

"That's the second reason I brought you here. I wanted you to see the proof that the syndicate's fortune was rightfully taken. Incidentally, in case you're wondering, Swiss banking authorities are required to provide information about secret accounts if there's substantial evidence showing those accounts are owned by criminal elements."

Dia had to sit down. She sank slowly into the nearest chair, a dazed look on her face. FIFASA, drug rings, Swiss bank accounts, seized billions—it was all happening so fast, and she, Lydia Fenner from Chillicothe, Ohio, was a part of it!

She looked up at him. "Jim, I don't know what to say. This is all so James Bondish. Is this for real? This isn't one of those elaborate practical jokes like they show on TV." Dia was half expecting all the people in the room to turn around and yell, "Surprise, you've been had!"

"I can assure you, this is real, Dia. And, oh yea, you wanted to know the part you played. Well, I doubt any of this would have happened without you."

"Wha-a-t?" Dia stammered with disbelief.

"Your testimony at the Senate hearing today was crucial in convincing us something outside economics was at work. When you said the reaction in the financial markets to the Fed's actions was outside the bounds of any economic model, then we knew to look for other motives," Jim explained.

"So what was the drug syndicate doing?" Dia asked.

"They were emptying their secret account in Zurich and flooding the world market with Treasury securities just as the Fed was buying securities. They were effectively sopping up the extra dollars just at the time the Fed was trying to get those dollars into the economy," Jim answered.

"Oh, I see. They were countering the Fed's moves and consequently preventing interest rates from falling," Dia added. "But there's something I don't understand. The syndicate would lose money—big money—as a result. If they waited for interest rates to fall, the value of their Treasury securities would have increased. I would think drug syndicates would want to make money with their investments, just like everybody else."

"You'd think so," Jim replied as he handed Dia a cup of coffee. "But we don't think they were motivated by profits. Instead, it seems they were motivated by revenge. You see, Narone's brother was killed in a raid led by U.S. Special Forces last year. Embarrassing the administration and crippling our economic policy was his way of getting back at us."

Just then Dia had a horrible thought. "Do you think the syndicate wanted to hurt me?"

"I don't know for certain, but I didn't want to take that chance until FIFASA's operation was complete. That's why I had to use the cloak and dagger moves to bring you here after your Senate testimony."

"While we're on the matter of cloak and dagger, here's something else I'm confused about. How did Trachsel know about my draft report that included all the reservations over macroeconomic policy? Only Kasten saw it, and now, of course, I know you saw it. But how did Trachsel find out?"

"I really don't know exactly how Trachsel found out. He certainly didn't get it from me," Jim assured her. "But Washington is like one big slice of Swiss cheese. There are holes and leaks everywhere through which information flows. Nothing, and I mean nothing, can be kept secret for very long."

Dia remembered when Adam Kasten told her there were ways of finding anything, if you only knew where to look.

Dia felt ashamed of her negative thoughts about Jim. All this time he had been watching out for her and, in the end, trying to protect her from some very powerful, very bad people.

"I guess I owe you an apology then, and a big thanks, too." Dia reached out and hugged him.

As Jim hugged her back, he whispered, "From now on, I hope we won't have any more secrets."

26. CONFUSION

Jim had the limo drive Dia back to her residence. He stayed behind to wrap up FIFASA's operation. Dia's head was whirling as she reached the apartment, dropped the keys on the kitchen counter, and sunk onto the couch. Almost immediately, the phone rang. She stared at it for a moment, thinking it might be more media, and was tempted to let it ring. Wearily, she reached over to answer.

"Sweetie, you're there," the familiar voice said. "I'm so glad. You were absolutely marvelous on TV today." It was amazing how just hearing her mother's voice could still make it all better.

"Thanks, Mom, but my Senate testimony this morning was actually the calmest part of my day." Dia then told her mom about her kidnapping at the hands of Jim Sawyer, followed by her witness to the thwarting of the Narone-Casini plot to counter the Fed's policy moves. Her mother was riveted. She didn't interrupt, listening quietly until her daughter finished.

"My gosh, honey, are your OK?" Ava Fenner said. "That Jim Sawyer should be strung up and whipped for what he put you through."

"No, Mom, Jim was merely doing his job," Dia countered gently. "Plus, he was sincerely concerned about my safety."

"OK, if you say so. I'm just relieved you're safe. You know I worry. I really didn't think your job could end up being this dangerous."

"To be honest, Mom, I didn't think so either. But you know what? As I look back now that it's all over, today sure was exciting."

"I don't know if I'd call being bullied by a gasbag senator and then scared to my wit's end by a spy wannabe exciting," Ava protested. "But as I said before, the important thing is you're safe."

"I'm sure I'll be brought back down to earth tomorrow. I think what I need now is about ten hours of good, undisturbed sleep."

"I agree, sweetie," Ava replied. "We'll talk more later. Surely after you've single-handedly saved the government they'll give you some days off, and you can come home for a nice, long visit."

"I don't know," Dia answered with resignation in her voice. "After all this, maybe I won't even have a job. I could end up spending a lot of time at home."

"Well, that would be fine with me," Ava said. "You stop worrying. Go get some sleep now."

"I will, Mom. Talk to you later."

"Bye-bye, dear." They hung up together.

Not quite having enough energy to even head to the bedroom, Dia eased back on the couch and clicked on the TV to catch up on the news. A press conference was in progress with the head of FIFASA. She leaned forward to get a clearer look at the screen. Standing behind the agency chief was Jim!

"We have been monitoring the Narone-Casini syndicate for years and knew they had amassed billions in their Swiss bank account," said Wallace Timlin, FIFASA's director. He turned slightly to acknowledge Jim with a gesture of his hand. "Upon the advice of Agent Sawyer here, we stepped up our surveillance after the recent policy announcement by the Federal Reserve."

"Did you use any information from Dr. Fenner of the Treasury Department in making the decision to go after Narone and Casini?" shouted a reporter.

Dia blushed at the mention of her name. It was curious she could feel both satisfaction and embarrassment at the same time.

"Agent Sawyer relied on the knowledge and expertise of Dr. Fenner in understanding what could be expected to happen from a change in monetary policy. And yes, her Senate testimony this morning was critical in our decision to work with the Swiss in seizing the syndicate's account." Timlin replied.

"Did Dr. Fenner know the true identity of Agent Sawyer?" another reporter yelled.

"No, she didn't," Timlin answered, looking mildly annoyed. "Agent Sawyer was legitimately serving as an economist with the Treasury Department, but at the same time he was gathering information that would help FIFASA perform its mission."

I guess this means Jim will have to be reassigned, Dia surmised. *Too bad!*

Abruptly the picture changed from the press conference to the SBS network studios. Sherwood Ritman was anchoring. "We're now going to break away from our coverage of the FIFASA press conference and talk to someone who can help us understand what has transpired today and what it means for people like you and me." Looking appropriately serious, Ritman continued, "Live via satellite from Ithaca, New York, we are joined by Professor Garrett Foster, a nationally recognized expert in macroeconomic policy at Cornell University. Professor Foster, thanks for being with us."

"My pleasure, Sherwood, thanks for having me," answered Foster with his usual cheerful demeanor.

"Professor Foster, what do you make of the events of the last twenty-four hours, in which it was found the Narone-Casini syndicate was using its considerable resources to stymie the policies of the Federal Reserve? Has anything remotely similar happened before?" Ritman asked.

"Not to my knowledge, Sherwood. I've never seen anything like this. All this intrigue just goes to show you economic policy doesn't have to be as boring as everyone thinks. Maybe this will encourage more students to take economics," Foster said with a laugh.

Ignoring this attempt at humor, Ritman, with a slight frown, asked his next question. "Seriously, Professor Foster, with the Narone-Casini roadblock removed, will the Fed's and administration's economic policies now lead to prosperity for the country?"

Dia reached for the remote to turn up the volume so she could hear her mentor's answer.

Accurately sensing that Ritman was all business, Foster used his direct, professional tone. "I'm more confident the Federal Reserve's actions will give a boost to the economy than the temporary fiscal actions proposed by the administration. But, of course, easing monetary policy now runs the risk of higher inflation on down the road."

Exactly what I tried to tell Bowman and Kasten, Dia thought.

"Then what's the solution to permanent economic prosperity, Professor?" Ritman asked.

Foster knew this was an important question in front of such a large audience, so he chose his words carefully. "I don't think we can ensure permanent economic prosperity for everyone," he said. "We live in a very dynamic economy. Recessions will occasionally hit us, and they are caused by a variety of uncontrollable factors. Something may spook consumers and cause them to lose confidence and dramatically curtail their spending. Or, businesses may overestimate consumer buying and have to cut back production and lay off workers. Conversely, there could be a supply crunch for some key input in the economy, like oil, which increases costs and slows production. Last, some economists argue that constantly changing government tax and spending policies causes even greater ripples in our economy."

"It sounds like you're pessimistic about the economy." Although Ritman sounded serious, his eyes indicated he was happy with where Foster had taken the conversation. Ritman knew bad economic news attracted viewers.

"Not at all, Mr. Ritman," Foster said formally. "I'm actually an economic optimist. The good news is today's recessions are shorter and much less severe than in the past. As new inventions and technology change both what is made and how, new industries will constantly be created at the same time other industries expire. Some workers will be hurt by these changes, but for the vast majority of us, they create a rising standard of living. A flexible and top-notch educational system with assistance for those workers displaced by economic change is the key to making our prosperity as widespread as possible."

To an economist like Dia, Foster's words were poetry.

Dia's thoughts were interrupted by the phone. She grabbed it with considerably more energy than before. Watching Garret Foster and listening to his words had given her an extra shot of energy.

"Hello."

"Hello, Dr. Fenner. This is Secretary Bowman's administrative assistant."

"Oh, hello, Tracy."

"Dr. Fenner, we all watched your testimony and then followed the unbelievable events afterward. Thank goodness, you weren't harmed."

"Thanks, Tracy. I wasn't so sure for a while what was happening and how things would end, but I was in good hands. I do appreciate your concern."

"All I can say is, you are one brave woman," offered Tracy. "Dr. Fenner, Secretary Bowman wanted to know if he could see you tomorrow—assuming you've recuperated enough. But if you need more time off, the Secretary understands."

"No, I feel fine, Tracy. Certainly I can meet with Secretary Bowman tomorrow."

"Great." Tracy sounded relieved. "Would nine tomorrow morning be OK?"

"Yes, that's fine. I'll be there."

"Thank you, Dr. Fenner. The Secretary will see you then. In the meantime, please call me if there's anything we can do for you. Good-bye, Dr. Fenner."

"Thank you, I will, Tracy. Good-bye."

Dia was puzzled. Clearly Tracy was acting on Bowman's orders. Why was he being so solicitous and gracious? Were the sentiments sincere, or were they window dressing prior to firing her? Certainly Trachsel was angry at Dia. Maybe Bowman and Trachsel had worked out a deal where Dia was sacrificed in exchange for Trachsel supporting the administration's fiscal policy proposals in Congress.

Feeling exhausted again, Dia headed for bed. With all these questions swirling in her head, she wasn't sure sleep would come easily. Only one thing was sure. Dia would know the answers tomorrow morning.

27. THE OFFER

Standing quickly, Lawrence Bowman greeted Dia warmly as she entered his inner office.

"Dr. Fenner, thank you so much for coming. It's really good to see you again. Please sit." Bowman pulled out the chair for her.

"Thank you," Dia responded.

"I took the liberty of learning your favorite drink is green tea. I happen to have a pot brewing. Care for a cup?" Bowman headed for the credenza where the tea service sat.

"Why, yes, thank you, sir," Dia managed to say. She hadn't expected this kind of treatment. How had Bowman discovered her love of tea? Maybe he had contacted her mother or former colleagues at Cornell.

"Dr. Fenner—or may I call you Dia?" Bowman began.

"Why, yes, of course." She was still uncomfortable being on familiar terms with superiors like the Secretary of the Treasury, but Dia answered affirmatively just to please him.

"Dia," Bowman began, now sitting directly across from her. "I first want to thank you for your testimony yesterday in the Senate. I have to admit I enjoyed seeing Trachsel get his comeuppance, all due to you I might add. That thorn in the administration's side was certainly taken down a couple of notches."

"Thank you, sir. I just told the truth."

"Yes, of course you did, and I would have expected nothing less." Dia wondered if Bowman was being truthful. "And I also understand your testimony was instrumental in stopping this drug syndicate from working against our economic plan." Dia could see the corner of the *Washington Post* article describing Tuesday's events peaking out from under a pile of other newspapers on Bowman's desk.

"Thank you again, Mr. Secretary. I answered the questions directly, using my best understanding of how the macroeconomy works." Dia couldn't help wishing Bowman would stop being so nice and just get on with the purpose for the meeting.

"I also want to apologize for not giving due consideration to your obvious considerable knowledge about both the possibilities and limits of policy," Bowman continued.

"That's very kind of you, Secretary Bowman." Dia thought some kind of answer was warranted.

"Which brings me to a personnel matter." Bowman leaned forward in his chair.

Ah, here it comes, thought Dia. *I'm gone*! She was beginning to understand things in the working world usually had more to them than one initially perceived. Dia held her breath as Bowman spoke.

"Adam Kasten has decided to pursue private opportunities outside of government. Adam joined the administration with me, but he had only planned to stay for a couple of years. I'm sure he'll do well in the private sector."

Dia exhaled, temporarily relieved. She wondered if Kasten really had left voluntarily, or was Bowman's merely sugarcoating to cover up Kasten's firing. Never the matter, she hoped her new boss would be an improvement—unless she was going to get the boot next.

"Now, Dia," Bowman said, his hands clasped in front of him, "in a very short period of time you have proven yourself to be a loyal and valuable member of the Treasury Department. Therefore, I'd like *you* to take Adam's position as Assistant Secretary for economic policy. You will have complete authority over the economics staff in the department. Of course, you'll report directly to me and participate with me in meetings at the White House. And, I might add, you'll receive a considerable upward adjustment in your salary." Bowman looked straight into Dia's eyes.

This was the last thing Dia had expected! Wasn't it only last night she had worried about being fired? In fact, her job had seemed to hang by a thread virtually the entire time she had been at Treasury. Now she was being offered one of the top economic positions in the entire federal government!

"Of course, you'll need Senate confirmation for this position," Bowman added. "I'm anticipating this will just be a formality given your indispensable role in ending our financial crisis. I suspect even our friend Senator Trachsel will support you." He winked at Dia.

28. THE NEW JOB

Dia sat at her new desk, in her new office, with a view she never dreamed she'd have. She had gotten in the habit of reading the *Washington Post* every morning to keep informed of the city's latest gossip. A front-page headline announced that Harriet Hagerty had just been nominated by the President for another term as Federal Reserve chairperson.

A letter from Kyle also lay on her desk. It had arrived several days earlier, and Dia had initially avoided even opening it. Rereading the letter, Dia thought of how many of her fears it explained away.

Kyle apologized for the threats he had made. He had wanted to get back at Dia for the breakup, and his stupid remark about "ruining her life" was an empty threat made in anger. He had never even come to Washington.

Their meeting in Virginia happened completely by chance. It was one of those unbelievable "small world" moments. Kyle had been on his way to North Carolina when he saw Dia at the gas station. Feeling so guilty about the way he had acted, he only wanted to apologize in person. That's why he followed her. Kyle got scared when he saw Dia stopped by the Virginia State Police. He thought Dia was going to have him arrested for threatening and stalking her. What a mixed-up mess of misinterpreted intentions—on both their parts!

Kyle was now working at a large organic farming operation in North Carolina, pursuing his dream of growing food with no chemical additives. He had read about Dia in the national press and said how proud he was of her. He closed by wishing her the best and hoped they could still be friends.

Dia was happy that chapter of her life was over. Now she was beginning a fresh one with different responsibilities. Today would be her first public appearance in her new job. She had butterflies.

Dia took long, deep breaths as she walked down the hallway to the meeting room. She didn't know what to expect. She had been up late last night preparing. She thought she had anticipated most of the possible questions, but she wasn't sure. She knew many people were counting on her, and she didn't want to disappoint them. Oh well, she'd just do the best she could.

As Dia entered the room, she could feel the sea of eyes focus on her. The chatting stopped. Some pulled out pens and pencils, others fired up their laptops, and a few positioned tape recorders to capture Dia's every word.

Standing in the front of the room, Dia cleared her throat and began to speak, "Good morning, I'm Dr. Fenner, and thank you for coming."

Unknown faces were trained on her.

Dia started her speech. "The macroeconomy is vitally important, because it has impacts on each of us. Factors like inflation, interest rates, the availability of jobs, taxes, government spending, and budget deficits are all elements of the macroeconomy. Yet individually we may feel powerless to understand the macroeconomy. As a business person, you may be doing everything right according to management principles, yet you're losing money because the macroeconomy is in a recession. Or you may be a thrifty person, saving a substantial part of your income, only to have some of the savings wiped out by a crash in the stock market or a jump in inflation."

"Yes," Dia pointed to her first questioner.

"Did you bring the syllabus today?"

"Yes, I did," Dia replied as she gave the two closest students bundles of the syllabus for distribution. "Anyway, these are only some of the issues we will address this semester in Introduction to Macroeconomics. We will cover both the theory and working of the macroeconomy as well as the practical applications of macroeconomic policy. And I promise you, I'll have plenty of personal tales to tell."

Several students giggled.

As the syllabus was passed out to the nineteen- and twenty-year-olds, Dia glanced out the window and gave a small wave as she saw Jim pull away from the parking space. She happily anticipated even more stories to share with her classes in the semesters to come.

NOTES

CHAPTER 4: FRIEND OR FOE?

There are two trade flows between countries measured by economists. The *current account* measures the trade in products and services between countries. The United States runs a *current account surplus* if the export of products and services from the States to other countries exceed the imports of goods and services from other countries. Conversely, the United States runs a *current account deficit* if the imports of goods and services from other countries to the States are greater than the exports of goods and services from the United States to other countries.

The *capital account* measures investment flows between countries. The United States has a *capital account surplus* if the amount of funds invested by foreigners in the U.S. exceeds the amount of funds invested by U.S. citizens in foreign countries. The U.S. runs a *capital account deficit* if the amount of funds invested by U.S. citizens in foreign countries is larger than the amount of funds invested by foreigners in the U.S.

Jim's statement that "investment flows to the U.S. are virtually the mirror image of the trade balance in goods and services" means the sum of the current account balance and the capital account balance will be zero. That is, if the current account is in deficit, it will be offset by a surplus in the capital account, and if the current account is in surplus, it will be countered by a deficit in the capital account.

In essence, if the U.S. imports more goods and services than it exports, it "pays" for the deficit by selling investments like stocks, bonds, buildings, and land.

The greatest manufacturing jobs losses have occurred in textiles and apparel, which are among the lowest paying of manufacturing industries.

The estimate of $20 billion in annual savings to domestic consumers of clothing is from Michael L. Walden, *Smart Economics: Commonsense Answers to 50 Questions About Government, Taxes, Business, and Households*, Praeger Publishing, 2005, Chp. 27.

CHAPTER 6: SHOT DOWN

More technical and detailed explanations of the concepts in this chapter can be found in any standard economics textbook, such as Arthur O'Sullivan and Steven M. Sheffrin, *Economics: Principles and Tools, 4th Edition*, Pearson Prentice-Hall, 2006.

CHAPTER 7: THE SUMMIT MEETING

Two excellent and highly readable accounts of the operation of the Federal Reserve are William Greider, *Secrets of the Temple: How the Federal Reserve Runs the Country*, Simon and Schuster, 1989; and Bob Woodward, *Maestro: Greenspan's Fed and the American Boom*, Simon and Schuster, 2000.

For a cinematic portrayal of a bank panic, see the Jimmy Stewart movie, *It's a Wonderful Life*, Republic Studios, 1947.

CHAPTER 8: DATE WITH THE ENEMY?

In the evaluation of many economists, the two leading economists of the twentieth century were John Maynard Keynes and Milton Friedman. As Dia explains, Keynes largely developed the policy tools governments use today to counter the business cycle. Conversely, Friedman has been highly critical of such interventionist policy.

Keynes's classic 1936 book is *The General Theory of Employment, Interest and Money* (Prometheus Books, 1997, reprint edition). Although the book is valuable, Keynes's writing style is not very readable. Fortunately, Friedman has written several popular, very accessible books outlining his ideas, including 1962's *Capitalism and Freedom* (University of Chicago, 2002, 40th anniversary edition) and 1980's *Free to Choose* (Harcourt, 1990, reprint edition).

CHAPTER 9: RESPITE

The difference between the payroll and household employment reports was apparent during the 2004 U.S. presidential campaign. The incumbent George W. Bush, running for reelection, used the household report to argue jobs had increased during his first term. Bush's opponent, Senator John Kerry, cited payroll report numbers to claim just the opposite—that jobs had decreased over the same period. Unfortunately, during their face-to-face debates in the fall of 2004, neither candidate challenged the other to explain the apparently contradictory statements.

The French unemployment is typically twice as high as the U.S. unemployment rate.

CHAPTER 13: BIRTH OF MONEY

Just as too much money growth can lead to inflation, too little money growth can lead to deflation, or the fall in prices. While declining prices may appear attractive on the surface, they carry two disadvantages. First, as Dia mentions in Chapter 22, wages and salaries would also fall, although this may not result in a lower standard of living if the decline in wages and salaries simply matched the decline in prices. Second, debt payments specified in set dollar amounts become relatively more expensive when prices fall and the effective purchasing power of the dollar rises.

Prices in the U.S. fell at the end of the nineteenth century when the country was on a gold standard, and gold supplies (and hence, the money supply) didn't keep pace with economic growth. Debtors, and particularly farmers, were hard hit by collapsing prices for their crops and livestock.

A little-known fact is that the children's book, *The Wizard of Oz*, published in 1900, is really a satire about the gold standard and falling prices between 1880 and 1900. Rural and farm groups wanted silver added to the money standard so the money supply would expand and prices would rise. In the book, "Oz" is the abbreviation for an ounce of gold, and the yellow brick road represents the gold standard. The book's heroine, Dorothy, is finally saved by her *silver* slippers (in the movie, the silver slippers were changed to ruby ones). For a complete economic interpretation of *The Wizard of Oz*, see Hugh Rockoff, "*The Wizard of Oz* as a Monetary Allegory," *Journal of Political Economy*, vol. 98, no. 4, 1990, pp. 739–760.

CHAPTER 18: SEEKING HELP

Professor John Seater of North Carolina State University has extensively examined the idea that businesses and households will increase their saving when a budget deficit occurs in anticipation of higher future taxes. His publications include:

"Are Future Taxes Discounted?" *Journal of Money, Credit, and Banking*, vol. 14, August 1982, pp. 376–389; "Does Government Debt Matter? A Review," *Journal of Monetary Economics*, vol. 16, July 1985, pp. 121–131; and "Ricardian Equivalence," *Journal of Economic Literature*, vol. 11, July 1993, pp. 265–277.

The "good empirical studies" to which Professor Foster refers include those by John Seater as well as the following: Paul Evans, "Interest Rates and Expected Future Budget Deficits in the U.S.," *Journal of Political Economy*, vol. 95, February 1987, pp. 34–58; Paul Evans, "Do Budget Deficits Raise Nominal Interest Rates? Evidence from Six Countries," *Journal of Monetary Economics*, vol. 20, Sept. 1987, pp. 281–300; Paul Evans, "Is Ricardian Equivalence a Good Approximation?" *Economic Inquiry*, vol. 29, October 1991, pp. 626–644; Robert Barro, "The Ricardian Approach to Budget Deficits," *Journal of Economic Perspectives*, vol. 3, spring 1989, pp. 37–54; and Roger Kormendi, "Government Debt, Government Spending, and Private Sector Behavior," *American Economic Review*, vol. 73, December 1983, pp. 994–1010.

Some economists have found a positive link between *forecasts* of budget deficits and *forecasts* of interest rates. See Thomas Laubach, "New Evidence on the Interest Rate Effects of Budget Deficits and Debt," Working Paper, Board of Governors of the Federal Reserve System, Washington, D.C., May 2003.

CHAPTER 20: IN HIDING

Buying "more house for the money" at more remote locations is a popular way of describing the economic concept of the "rent gradient." Sites closer to centers of economic activity are more costly because of their advantage of accessibility. Households will choose residential locations depending on their preferences for accessibility versus housing space.

In 2005 the U.S. Supreme Court ruled that states could not prohibit direct sales of out-of-state wineries while allowing such sales for instate wineries.

Another major issue in measuring inflation is how to account for quality changes in some products. For example, if next year all vehicles come equipped with side air bags as standard equipment, and if this feature adds $300 to a vehicle's price, we wouldn't want to consider the $300 as part of inflation, because it was paid to get something new and better. That is, inflation only refers to price changes for the same products with the exact same features and characteristics.

But because product features and characteristics are constantly changing, it takes government economists a great deal of time and effort to make sure the official inflation rate measures only "apple-to-apple" price changes and not "apple-to-orange" changes.

CHAPTER 24: TAKEN

Under certain conditions, some macroeconomic models could predict a rise in interest rates when the Fed increases the money supply. This could happen if financial markets immediately anticipated a sufficient rise in the inflation rate as a result of the Fed's actions, and this higher inflation rate immediately pushed up interest rates. However, such conditions appear not to be present in the U.S. economy.

CHAPTER 25: FINAL FEAR

To the authors' knowledge, FIFASA is a fictitious agency.

CHAPTER 26: CONFUSION

Understanding the causes of recessions remains one of the key areas of economic study. During the long growth periods of the 1980s and 1990s, there was much speculation that recessions were a phenomenon of the past. But then, recessions hit the economy in the early 1990s and early 2000s.

The last two recessions of 1990–91 and 2001 were shorter and milder than previous recessions. The 1990–91 and 2001 recessions each lasted eight months, during which the economy contracted an average of 1 percent. In contrast, the eight recessions between 1948 and 1982 lasted an average of eleven months and the economy shrank an average of 2.6 percent.

The potential reasons for the reduction in the duration and severity of recessions are varied and include the movement of economic activity from the more volatile manufacturing sector to the less volatile service sector and more effective antirecession policies.

Made in the USA